SURFEIT
OF SUSPECTS

SURFEIT
OF SUSPECTS

GEORGE BELLAIRS

with an introduction by
MARTIN EDWARDS

This edition published 2019 by
The British Library
96 Euston Road
London NW1 2DB

Originally published in 1964 by John Gifford, London

Cataloguing in Publication Data
A catalogue record for this book is available from the British Library

ISBN 978 0 7123 5238 3
eISBN 978 0 7123 6484 3

Front cover image © NRM/Pictorial Collection/
Science & Society Picture Library

Typeset by Xxxxxx, London
Printed in England by CPI Group (UK) Ltd, Croydon, CR0 4YY

CONTENTS

INTRODUCTION   7

1. *Sky High*   11
2. *Dead Broke*   26
3. *Legal Advice*   36
4. *The Gatekeeper*   50
5. *Dynamite*   63
6. *Old Tom Hoop*   78
7. *Overdrafts*   92
8. *Polydore*   106
9. *Takeover*   126
10. *Pook's Retreat*   147
11. *Bugler Scared*   158
12. *Surfeit of Suspects*   172
13. *Dynamite Disappears*   182
14. *Directors' Meeting*   194
15. *Account Rendered*   206

INTRODUCTION

Surfeit of Suspects begins with a bang. Literally: in the first paragraph, 'a terrific explosion' destroys the premises of the Excelsior Joinery Company. In the third, it emerges that three people have been killed in the blast. George Bellairs' novels are sometimes described as low-key, but such an opening to a story is as dramatic as any thrill-seeker could wish for.

The dead men are three of the five directors of the company, and it quickly becomes apparent that the explosion was no accident. Did someone target the directors – or one of them – or was the aim to destroy a business which was already in financial jeopardy? Or was there a subtler motive? It's a case for Scotland Yard, in the shape of Superintendent Tom Littlejohn and his trusty sidekick, Inspector Cromwell.

The scene of the crime is in Evingden, in Surrey. Not so long ago, it was a small, sleepy place where everybody knew everybody else; now, it's growing rapidly. Littlejohn finds himself confronted with intrigue aplenty, including a recent abortive attempt to rob a bank, and the clues include scrawled notes on a piece of paper that one of the deceased was clutching in his hand. All is ultimately revealed when Littlejohn assembles the suspects in a solicitor's office. Financial shenanigans play a part in the storyline, and George Bellairs clearly drew on his personal knowledge of business life in constructing the plot.

George Bellairs was a pseudonym. The author's real name was Harold Blundell (1902–82), and although he was himself a bank manager, he found time to write no fewer than fifty-eight Bellairs novels from 1941 onwards. R. F. Stewart, who wrote an entertaining article about Bellairs in the fanzine CADS, speculated that his forename was a hat-tip to French crime writer Georges Simenon. Simenon's series detective Jules Maigret is, like Bellairs' detective Littlejohn, a humane, uxorious man with a fondness for smoking a pipe, rather than a cerebral reasoning machine; however, the similarities can't be pressed too far, and Freeman Wills Crofts' meticulous Inspector Joseph French perhaps bears a closer resemblance to Littlejohn. In any event, the author said that the pen-name was based on the initials of his wife – Gwladys Blundell.

The publishing business was very different in Bellairs' time, although some things don't change. He was modestly – *very* modestly – remunerated for his efforts, but at least he had the satisfaction of remaining in print (in hardback; few of his novels made it into paperback editions) for almost forty years. Today, authors may, if they are lucky, benefit from much greater investment and (sometimes) marketing, but if their books fail to earn an adequate return, they are soon likely to find themselves dropped from their publisher's list, a fate which, in the UK, never befell Bellairs. Because he was able to live on his earnings from Martins Bank, he enjoyed the luxury of writing to amuse himself, while giving occasional talks about his work and writing newspaper articles to earn pocket money. His lifestyle seems to have been agreeable, and on his retirement, he and Gwladys moved to the Isle of Man, a place they loved and which served as the setting for many of his stories.

After 1952, his books ceased to be published in the US; reading tastes there had changed, and more highly charged stories from newcomers such as Ross Macdonald and Patricia Highsmith had come into vogue. Compensation came from across the Channel, as Littlejohn found particular favour with French readers; the books were often retitled to include the detective's surname, rather in the fashion of the Maigret stories. Bellairs was published in other European countries, and also in Mexico and South America. He reckoned that of his readers 'over 50 percent are old ladies who like murder and more murder, but jib at extreme violence on the part of the police', and he took care not to antagonise them. Settings mattered to him, and (like John Bude, another author whose books appear in the British Library's Crime Classics series) he made a virtue of writing mysteries – *Death in High Provence* is an example – based in appealing locations.

R. F. Stewart rightly emphasises Bellairs' other strengths, namely humour and concise characterisation: 'The humour is of the quiet, wry variety. The characterisation is not by way of slow development but in thumbnail sketches… we are given amusing little pen-pictures of people whom Littlejohn meets in the course of his enquiries and whom we suspect Bellairs of having actually met in the course of his life. Policemen, clerics and solicitors are among his favourites for poking fun at, but especially bank managers, on whom Bellairs was by definition an authority.' In this novel, one of the key characters is a hapless bank manager who rejoices in the name George Frederick Handel Roper.

The book was published during the Swinging Sixties, though – despite fleeting reference to teddy-boys and pop singers – you might be forgiven for not guessing it from the text. P. D. James and Ruth Rendell had just arrived on the scene, and the nature of crime fiction in Britain was evolving, as it had done in the US. Even in 1964, *Surfeit of Suspects* must have seemed a little old-fashioned to many of the library users who constituted Bellairs' principal readership. But there is comfort and pleasure to be had in the familiar, and more than half a century after its original appearance, this novel remains an amiable read, light entertainment which gives us a glimpse of a long-vanished world, a world that was already vanishing even as Bellairs wrote about it.

MARTIN EDWARDS
www.martinedwardsbooks.com

I

SKY HIGH

At eight o'clock in the evening on the 8th of November, there was a terrific explosion in Green Lane, Evingden. It smashed all the windows of two rows of terraced cottages in the vicinity and the front of a corner shop completely collapsed and strewed sweets and provisions all over the pavement. When the startled tenants of the damaged houses rushed outside, they found the offices of the Excelsior Joinery Company reduced to a mass of rubble.

It was some time before the bewildered occupants of Green Lane thought of sending for the police. They didn't quite realise what had happened. They were suffering from concussion and it took them a little while to get over it. They thought of bombs, fireworks, gas-mains and gunpowder. Even those trained in civil defence had to shake off the nightmare and made a late start in functioning.

Meanwhile, the wrecked building, illuminated by a broken gas-main which had become ignited and spread a yellow hissing glow over the ruins, continued to disintegrate, shedding loose bricks, plaster and timber which soon started to burn. Someone telephoned for the fire brigade and the police and only then did one of the lookers-on suddenly proclaim in a shrill voice that there was a body in the debris. Three men with more initiative and guts than the rest rushed to recover it before the flames spread. Instead of returning with a single corpse, the rescuers emerged with one apiece.

'They've all had it,' said a man called Prime, who was the Johnny-know-all of Green Lane. And this time he was right.

Normally, Green Lane was a quiet street on the edge of the town. It had been green once, but now trees and other vegetation which struggled to appear in the summer time were quickly coated with the white dust of passing traffic or with soot poured down from the numerous chimneys of the vicinity. On one side of the street which joined together the two main thoroughfares like the bar across a letter H, were two blocks of terraced houses and the large factory of the Excelsior Joinery Company. On the other side, the huge timber-yard of the company, and its registered office stood on an island site. For a couple of hours after the explosion the local fire brigade was kept on its toes preventing the flames from spreading from the office to the timber-yard.

Sergeant Jeal and two of his men didn't need to ask where the fire was. As they left the police-station they could see the glow of it in the sky and found themselves borne along by the stream of townspeople turning out to see what was happening. As a rule Green Lane was silent after dark, shadowy and haunted-looking under its gas lamps. Sergeant Jeal now found it packed from end to end with a motley crowd, faces like masks under the glow of the fire and almost talking in whispers because the news of the deaths had got around.

'What's goin' on?' said Jeal as he and his retinue shouldered their way through the mob.

The sight of the helmets brought the ubiquitous Mr. Prime in their direction right away. He was overflowing with information. He told of the explosion, volunteered his opinion as to how it had occurred – 'faulty gas-main, that's wot it was' – and offered to conduct the police to where the bodies had been placed.

'Funny thing, the explosion doesn't seem to have been wot killed 'em. Either the ceilin' fell-in on 'em, or else they was brained by failin' bricks and timber... They look quite peaceful...'

'Who are they?'

Mr. Prime, a little thin sallow man with a pair of imitation tortoiseshell spectacles held together by cotton wound around the nosepiece, had to shout to make himself heard above the noise of the crowd and the firemen.

'John Willie Dodd, Dick Fallows and John Robert Piper. They were directors of the Excelsior and must 'ave been havin' a meetin' in the office. Lucky the other two directors weren't there. Tom Hoop, the chairman's in bed with 'flu, and Fred Hoop hadn't turned up at the meetin'...'

Mr. Prime turned to look at the fire again and shook his head.

'The Hoops'll be sorry they stopped the fire from gettin' at the timber...'

Sergeant Jeal who'd only been half listening to the spate of information suddenly turned on Prime.

'What's that you're saying?'

Mr. Prime shouted louder than ever.

'The 'oops'll be sorry the timber-yard's not goin' up in smoke, too. The Excelsior's as good as bust... Bankrupt, if you know wot I mean...'

'I know what you mean, but...'

Sergeant Jeal turned to address Mr. Prime again and discovered he'd vanished. In the ebb and flow of the struggling crowd, he'd been caught-up and carried off by a current, like a poor swimmer going out with the tide.

Sergeant Jeal found himself at a bit of a loss. The first thing he felt he ought to do was to clear away the milling crowds, but he'd only two bobbies to fall back on and it was quite beyond their capacity. A huge, red-faced man, he felt he could have disposed of the mob by instalments, two or three at a time, but there were nearly two hundred of them at a guess... Jeal sighed with relief when he saw the hat of Inspector Tattersall approaching him, like a cork floating across the sea of heads. It was a rather rakish cloth hat, with a feather in the band.

Tattersall had been off duty and had just been enjoying a Western with his wife in the local cinema, when he had received a message, superimposed on the screen across the Great Salt Desert (wherever that might be!) over which the sheriff was shambling with a captured outlaw.

> *If Inspector Tattersall is in the audience will he report at the box office. Thank you.*

It looked as if the thirst-racked man wearing a tin star needed a bit of official help.

'Don't forget to put your scarf on,' said Mrs. Tattersall and settled down to watch the film through on her own.

Tattersall was wearing his scarf when he arrived on the scene. It was beginning to rain. It seemed to cheer him up. He was a tall, thin man, with a long face and a heavy nose. An imperturbable sort, he'd not even complained about being called from the pictures, although he hadn't thought it a bit funny when some of the audience began to laugh and cheer at the announcement. He looked hard at Jeal's deadpan face.

'Good evening, Jeal.'

Jeal swallowed heavily and the strap under his chin rose and fell. 'Good evening, sir.'

He said it in an apologetic voice and added 'I'm sorry,' for he knew Tattersall's weakness for Wild West films.

'Sorry for what? You didn't start the fire, did you?'

'No, sir. It's more than a fire. There's three dead men in it, as well.'

It sounded like the film Tattersall had just left. Three dead men in Boot Hill, instead of in the timber-yard gatehouse.

'How far have you gone?'

'I've not even seen the bodies yet, sir. We've only just arrived ourselves, and this mob...'

'The rain'll soon shift 'em. Tell them to make way.'

The morale of the crowd was already faltering under the growing weight of rain, which competed with the firemen in putting out the blaze. The police found the passage to the gatehouse easy now.

It was a two-storeyed wooden building with a tin roof and a weighing machine outside the door. Illuminated by a single bare electric bulb and covered by one huge tarpaulin sheet were the three bodies, guarded by the gateman who was smoking thick-twist. The small room was full of acrid tobacco smoke.

The man put down his pipe and drew back the sheet. He had a hook where his left hand should be. Tattersall regarded the three victims without a word, after removing the famous hat. Someone had straightened them out and laid them in an orderly row. All seemed to have died in the same way. A falling beam or bricks must have smashed in their heads, which were not a pretty sight. Tattersall pursed his lips. He'd been through some nasty scenes in the war, but violent death always turned him up a bit.

'Cover them up again...'

The gatekeeper hooked back the tarpaulin and stood eagerly waiting for the oracle to speak. Jeal stood behind Tattersall

breathing heavily and his two attendant coppers brought up the
rear, standing to attention.

'Well, lads, don't stand there on parade. One of you go and bring
the chief fire officer to me. I suppose he's with the brigade by now...'

Garnett, the head of the fire brigade, had been in the cinema
as well, but had made a hell-for-leather exit when he heard the
clanging fire engine, its noise drowning the shots of a gunfight,
passing the door.

A constable hurried out.

'You better ring Dr. Stephens, Jeal. Tell him to hurry. We've
three bodies here for him. And then, telephone the station, advise
that there's been a fatal fire in Green Lane, and get them to ring
the forensic people and ask them to come here as soon as they can.
Say there's been an explosion and three deaths and we're eager to
know what it's all about.'

The remaining bobby, a young chap not long in the force, was
beginning to think he'd been forgotten.

'Constable Forrest, isn't it?'

'Yes sir.'

'Well, until the sergeant returns, you're in charge of the scene
of the fire. The rain and the brigade will soon have the thing under
control and then the snoopers will be around seeing what they can
find and carry off. You're to see they're kept away.'

'Yes, sir.'

As Forrest went out he passed Garnett on his way in. A stocky
man with a grim craggy face which had been blackened by smoke
and burnt wood.

'Enjoy the pictures, Garnett?'

'No, I didn't. I knew when the missus wanted to go there'd be
a fire as soon as we got settled. Were you there?'

'Yes. I'll have to ask my wife to tell me how it ended. This is a mess, isn't it?'

'Yes. It's an old building and the wood's as dry as a bone. As soon as the flame spouted from the gas-fire, the whole lot went up like a rocket.'

'There was an explosion first?'

'You're tellin' me. It blew all the windows out in the houses opposite.'

'Gas?'

'No. There were only two gas-fires in the building, fed by a narrow inlet from the street main. It was something worse. To my way of thinking there must have been some powerful explosive in the office that went off. What it was doing there I can't think. You don't use stuff like blasting powder for joinery work.'

'We'll have to wait until the experts get on it then. Meanwhile, I'd better get hold of some of the officials of the company and have a talk with them. Where are they all?'

'Most of them are under the tarpaulin there, Tattersall. Three directors. There was a meeting going on when it all happened. I hear that the Chairman, Tom Hoop, and his son, Fred, the managing director, were absent. Old Tom's in bed with the flu. I don't know where Fred is. Nobody seems to know. His wife's away from home and the place is locked up. He lives on the edge of the town; Burgoyne Road. I only hope they don't find Fred among the ashes as well.'

'Where's the Chairman live?'

'Two streets away from here. They tell me he hasn't been told about this affair. If he had been, he'd have got up from bed if he'd been dying. He's too ill to be disturbed.'

'You seem very well informed, Garnett.'

'When you're working on a fire, you hear some funny things. The flames seem to mesmerise people and make them talk more freely. Some of them become quite indiscreet... I'd better be getting back to the fire. You'll see that as little as possible is disturbed...'

Garnett's mouth opened wide in astonishment and the whites of his eyes shone in his blackened face. 'Disturbed! Can you tell me anythin' more disturbing than an explosion followed by a fire? The place is a shambles. Bricks, rubble, burning wood and papers. Water everywhere. You'll be lucky.'

'Keep your shirt on. I only want the experts who're on their way here to find out what caused it all, if they can.'

'Good luck to them, too. Are you imagining it was a put-up job?'

'One never knows.'

The doctor arrived as they were leaving and insisted on Tattersall returning with him. A little peppery man with a red nose and wearing a dinner jacket under his overcoat. He gave the three victims a cursory examination.

'They brought me out of my lodge meeting to attend to these. They've been dead some time.'

He indicated the bodies.

'What good can I do? The cause of death is obvious. They were killed by falling masonry or the like... We'll have them moved to the mortuary. Fix it up, will you, Tattersall? Get an ambulance along. I'll go into things properly tomorrow and do a post-mortem on them. Good night.'

Just like that! He was off back to his lodge.

Outside, it was raining cats and dogs. They could hear the doctor swearing at the weather and then shunting his car and hooting soaked spectators out of the way. From the distance came the vigorous tapping of many hammers. Already people were boarding-up their damaged windows with cardboard and planks from the joinery works.

Running feet and another sopping specimen entered the gate-house. He seemed unaffected by the weather, although water was dropping from his felt hat and he looked as though they'd hooked him from the river.

Fred Hoop. He was so like a drowned rat that Tattersall hardly recognised him.

'Good evening, Mr. Hoop.'

Hoop was too busy to return the courtesy.

'What's going on here?'

'Isn't that obvious?'

Fred Hoop was tall and slim, with a thin nose like a scythe and a long face with a streak of dark moustache across his upper lip. A machinist, suddenly promoted to be managing director, he was touchy and bombastic.

'I don't want any lip from the police. I want to know what's happened and who...'

Then he saw the tarpaulin.

'What's that?'

'Three bodies from the fire.'

Hoop made as if to uncover them and Tattersall held him back.

'That will do no good. Fallows, Piper and Dodd. It seems they were holding a meeting when the explosion occurred...'

'Explosion? What the hell's been going on?'

'Don't you know what's been happening to your own business, Mr. Hoop? Where have you been all the evening?'

Tattersall looked at his watch. It was 11.23.

'That's no business of yours.'

'But it is. There are three dead men lying there. Their deaths have to be accounted for. The fire at your company's offices started with a loud explosion. We don't know what caused it, but experts are on their way to investigate it. Meanwhile, we've our own side of the investigation to make and I'll begin with you, sir. Where have you been all night?'

Hoop took off his hat and shook the water from it. It didn't seem to have occurred to him to bare his head in the presence of his three dead colleagues. Then he took off his spectacles and dried the water from them on his scarf. His eyes were dark and shifty and moved rapidly here and there as though he suspected listeners hidden behind the piles of sacks and packing cases littered about the room.

'I called to see my father, who's ill with flu. He's in bed and very poorly.'

'You haven't been there all night, have you?'

'No. I'm coming to it if you'll let me. I left my father's at about seven o'clock and went home. My wife has gone to her mother's at Brantwood, so after I'd been home and made myself a cup of tea, I went to bring my wife back. When I got there they were having a meal and I joined them. About nine o'clock somebody called to say there was a fire at the works. They said they hadn't been able to find me before. I hurried here right away. I thought the lot had gone up in smoke. Instead, it was just the office and the fire had been put out.'

He sounded disappointed.

'It seems there might have been a meeting of the directors going on tonight when the explosion occurred, Mr. Hoop.'

'There was no meeting called and don't you be thinking I've had anything to do with the fire. I know you're wondering why, if it was a directors' meeting, I wasn't there and it's entered your mind that I wasn't because I was going to start a fire…'

'Now, now, now, Mr. Hoop. I had no such thoughts. I simply asked if there was a directors' meeting…'

'Well, there wasn't. Those three must have been arranging something behind my back. I don't want to speak ill of them, and they lying there, but that's what it looks like…'

As though to ease his mind, two ambulance men arrived to take the bodies away. There was a policeman with them. They looked at the tarpaulin and one of them cocked an eye at Tattersall.

'Three?'

'Yes.'

'We've only brought two stretchers. Nobody told us there were three.'

'Well, make another out of the tarpaulin and get a move on. It's not decent leaving them lying here for hours.'

Everybody's nerves seemed to be frayed. Hoop tried to light a cigarette, but his matches were damp and he couldn't manage it. Tattersall flicked his lighter.

'Here, light it from this. We'll go outside while these men are doing their job.'

'It's time I was getting home. I'm wet through.'

Tattersall didn't answer but led the way out.

The rain had ceased and there was a damp, aromatic smell of timber on the air. The street lamps had gone out at eleven, but most of the houses in the vicinity had lights showing round the chinks of the boarded windows of the front downstairs rooms, where the occupants were presumably still discussing the night's events. In Green Lane there was an acrid smell of burnt wood. The fire had been put out, but firemen were still scrambling among the wreckage and spraying the smoking ruins with a single hosepipe. Most of the spectators had gone home and the persistent hammering had ceased. Here and there a small knot of men, who couldn't persuade themselves to leave, made a blacker shadow in the darkness of the street, hanging round extinguished street lamps as though, somehow, there was shelter there.

Sergeant Jeal appeared out of the gloom. The firemen had erected two electric lamps focused on the demolished offices and by the light of them Tattersall could see Jeal's red face lined with soot.

'The county experts are on their way, sir. They should be here within the next half-hour.'

'You'd better wait with your men until they're satisfied. I don't think they'll be able to do much in this light. If they want to leave it till daylight, put a couple of men on to see that nobody starts wandering about the ruins...'

Tattersall looked around for Hoop, who until now, had been at his elbow, following him like a dog.

'Where's Hoop?'

'I haven't seen him.'

Then they spotted him among the ruins, rambling disconsolately about, poking here and there with a piece of stick he'd picked up, bending to inspect the littered floors.

'Go and get him out of that, Jeal. He'll get hurt by falling bricks. We don't want another casualty. If he starts to argue, tell him the police have taken charge. Carry him out if he won't come under his own steam.'

Jeal squared himself and went to execute his orders.

Hoop didn't argue. A man without much guts, known to be dominated by his wife, but prone to fits of childish temper if he didn't get his own way. Now, he gave up without a word and joined Tattersall.

'What a mess. All the books have gone up in smoke and the safe's buried under a lot of bricks and mortar. I don't know how we'll start to clean up this lot. Lucky it didn't spread to the works and timber-yard. The men can, at least, make a start when they come in the morning. All the stock sheets and invoices have been burned too. I don't know...'

Tattersall was fed up with the steadily rising lamentations. It was beginning to rain again, too.

'You'd better be off home then, Mr. Hoop. I'll want to see you first thing in the morning, though. We'll go properly into matters then.'

'I'll be busy all day tomorrow. You'll appreciate that with three of the main men dead, a lot's going to fall on me. And with my father ill in bed. I don't know what'll happen when they tell him about all this.'

'I think you'd better call at the police station at ten in the morning, Mr. Hoop. We'll resume our talk then.'

'But...'

'Be there, sir. Three men have lost their lives in this fire and it started with an explosion. That puts it out of the normal run of such things. Good night.'

''night. Give me another light from your lighter. My matches are wet.'

In the light of the small pale flame, Hoop's features were dead white, his spectacles awry, his cheeks smeared with soot. He thrust forward his anxious face and pursed mouth to draw the flame to his cigarette. Then he went into the night without another word.

It was then that Tattersall realised that he hadn't enquired about the relatives of the victims. He sought out Sergeant Jeal, who had returned to the fire to post his men.

'What about the relatives? Were they informed?'

'Yes, sir. I did that myself. Things seem to be so much on top of us, I haven't had time to report. Fallows lost his wife a couple of years ago and lives with an old housekeeper in a small house just a couple of streets away. She seemed a bit stunned, but didn't shed any tears. I'm told his nearest relatives live somewhere in the neighbourhood. We'll have to contact them later. No... All she seemed really concerned about was how she was going to get another job at her age.'

'What about Dodd? He's a family man, isn't he?'

'Yes. Wife and two boys. They're away from home. Gone to see their relatives at the seaside... Anglesey. We've asked the police there to let Mrs. Dodd know. I expect she'll be back here as soon as there's a train. Piper was an older man, with a married daughter. His wife and him live on their own a few minutes' walk from here. Mrs. Piper took it bad. We got the doctor to her and then sent for her daughter. She's gone home with her daughter, who lives on the other side of town...'

'Thank you, Jeal, for looking after it. It's a bad business.'

Jeal nodded sympathetically. He looked like a circus bobby, with his helmet awry and dusty, his streaked face and his red-rimmed eyes. But there was nothing comic about him. He seemed to have acquired a new, sad dignity.

'I'll get back to the station, then. I don't suppose there'll be much sleep for any of us tonight. See you in the morning, Jeal.'

'Good night, sir.'

Tattersall made his way through the empty streets with pavements still wet and shining. Somewhere a clock struck two. Time seemed to have moved quickly. A car passed him travelling at speed and a dog began to bark.

Next morning he met the experts who'd already made a cursory examination of the ruins of the company's offices.

No doubt about it, the place had been blown sky-high with dynamite.

At noon, the matter was reported to Scotland Yard.

2

DEAD BROKE

'I SUPPOSE YOU'LL HAVE TO DISINTER THIS BEFORE YOU CAN pay the wages...'

Littlejohn kicked the corner of a large old-fashioned safe which protruded from the debris.

He said it more for something to break the tragic silence than anything else and tried to make his comment sound humorous. But he didn't succeed.

The little man standing beside him uttered a single syllable of contempt. '*Hé!*'

He was the company's book-keeper. A little chubby man, with a bald, orange-shaped head, flabby features and a pale pink complexion tinged with liverish yellow. He'd been up all night, wringing his hands at the disaster and there were dark bags under his eyes. He wore the symptoms of failure; a man who had probably started life with high hopes and ended in his late fifties as clerk in a bankrupt concern.

'What does it contain?'

'Old books. There's no cash in it. In fact, there's none about the place. We just scratched along, week after week, pleading with the bank for help to tide us over... Now, I guess it's finished. With Dodd dead and out of it, the business'll fold up.'

He chanted it to himself, like a sacristan busy with the litany. There were little flecks of foam at the corners of his mouth.

Tattersall had driven Littlejohn and Cromwell to the scene of the fire. He'd told them all there was to know, so far, and it wasn't much. Just that the experts were of the opinion that someone had touched off the whole affair with a stick of blasting-powder. They'd taken away one or two bits and pieces for examination and promised to report later. Tattersall had left the Scotland Yard men to browse over the ruins and gone to court, where he was due to prosecute a gang who'd broken in a bicycle shop and, unable to find any cash, had wrecked the place and ridden away with a bicycle apiece.

It was still raining. A cold drizzle which seemed to penetrate right to your bones. Green Lane, with its dark unkempt trees, looked a picture of misery. The police had driven away intruders and roped off the wreck left behind by the fire. The fire brigade had gone, leaving a mess of fallen bricks and rubble, with the burned wooden window frames, devoid of glass, mostly still in place. The whole building looked as if it had been hit by a bomb.

Jeal and a young policeman who followed him about like an acolyte, were drinking tea in the gatehouse of the timber-yard. There were two lorries there being loaded with finished joinery-work, doors, window frames and cupboards, all unpainted and ready for fixing somewhere in a building estate. Work went on quietly as though everybody's spirits had been stifled by the tragedy. Earlier in the day, Fred Hoop had arrived and laid off all the workmen of the factory. With Dodd out of the way, the mainspring seemed to have gone. Then, Hoop had taken himself off to see the insurance agent.

Bugler, the book-keeper, continued his lamentations, talking to himself, if nobody else would listen.

'I'm fed up. I've finished with this sort of work. The last place I was with went bust, too. I'm getting too old to keep being pushed around. After this, I'm trying a new line. My sister's husband,

Albert, runs a betting-shop in the town and I'm going in with him. Perhaps you've noticed the place. Albert Scriboma. No? We talked it over last night. "Ossie," Albert said, "Ossie, it's time you stopped workin' for people who pick your brains and then chuck you on the rubbish heap. It's time you started thinkin' of your future…" So…'

Scriboma. What a name! Littlejohn could imagine the melancholy Ossie among the optimistic punters.

Ossie took off his spectacles and slowly wiped the rain from them. Then he kicked the safe.

'So, I'm off.'

'Is there anywhere where we could have a talk? Somewhere where it's dry and warm?'

Ossie didn't seem surprised at the request. He nodded and shook the rain from his hat.

Littlejohn was fed up with scrambling about in the soggy ruins and was beginning to wish he'd accepted the gatekeeper's offer of a cup of tea.

'You can come over to my office, such as it is.'

Ossie's contempt for it was justified. He did his work in a shabby corner of the main workshop, glass-partitioned from the rest and heated by a small electric fire. The current had gone off in last night's commotion, and it was cold and damp. Outside stood a large planing machine, surrounded by piles of wood chippings and then three lathes covered in timber dust. The atmosphere seemed deadened by the mass of sawdust and shavings outside and when anyone spoke it sounded like a crypt.

There were two old wooden chairs in the room and Ossie told Littlejohn and Cromwell to sit down. He was in no mood for offering hospitality. He'd given up smoking and, in any event, smoking was forbidden among so much inflammable material. However, the young policeman arrived with three cups of tea, hot, strong and very sweet, on a plank of wood. The bobby was scared of Littlejohn and his huge hands trembled as he passed out the drinks. This was his first encounter with Scotland Yard and he had an idea that if he acquitted himself well, he might be promoted before long. As soon as he was free of his burden, he sprang to attention, saluted in enthusiastic sergeant-major fashion and said, 'Compliments of Sergeant Jeal, sir,' although Jeal had nothing to do with it. Then he briskly left them.

'Smart young chap,' said Cromwell. The young chap heard it as he shuffled through the shavings and it sustained him for a long time afterwards.

It was even more dismal here than in the open air. The whole place had a dejected look as though expecting to be burned down, too, at any time. Ossie sucked in his tea with a pouting mouth. He started his jeremiad again.

'I always said that…'

Littlejohn had had enough.

'I suppose this is the place where the books are kept and the main office work is done?'

'It was. The books were kept in that steel cabinet, and Dodd took them across to the office to look them over. They've gone up in smoke. They can't expect me to reconstruct them and produce a new set. The accountant who does the audit will have to do that. I'm not stopping on to do it. It would drive me up the wall.'

'What went on in the office that was burned down, then? You, I take it, did most of the official work here.'

'I didn't. The board-room was over there and the typist and type-writer as well. Dodd did all the correspondence. He was officially

the secretary, you see. He bought all the timber and dealt with all
the orders and cash and cheques… when there were any. Things
have been so bad of late that they could well have done without
me. But Mr. Dodd didn't like routine work, so I was kept on to
do it. I dealt with the books, the invoices, writing out cheques for
accounts for signatures when Dodd could persuade the bank to
pay them. And if the cheques bounced, I was the one who got the
abuse over the telephone.'

'Things were bad financially?'

'Never worse. Mind you, it wasn't always that way. When Mr.
Jonas owned the place, it did all right.'

'Mr. Jonas who?'

'Mr. Jonas. Henry Jonas. It was his family business. It once
employed over a hundred and fifty men. Now there are twenty-
five. Or *were*. Mr. Fred Hoop laid most of them off this morning,
and they'll be lucky if they ever start again…'

He cast his sad glaucous eyes on a framed picture askew on
the wall. It had apparently been taken years ago on some kind of
a works outing or jubilee. A crowd of workmen, all dressed in
their best, arranged in orderly rows by the photographer, with a
line of seated men in front – obviously the officials and adminis-
trators – and an elderly man, who couldn't have been anyone but
Mr. Jonas himself, legs crossed, proud and smiling, a king among
his subjects, with a torpedo beard like Captain Kettle. Happy days
for Excelsior!

'What was the set-up after Mr. Jonas left it?'

'He died. Quite suddenly, it happened. One minute he was
joking with one of the joiners. Next, he was dead among the shavings. Heart attack.'

'Did he own the whole of it?'

'He'd no son and Miss Eva and Miss Agnes, his daughters, were directors along with him. Not that they knew a thing about business, but it kept it in the family.'

'How long has Mr. Jonas been dead?'

'Five years. When he died his daughters removed to Bournemouth. Mrs. Jonas had been dead about ten years then. It looked as if the whole concern would come under the hammer. Then, John Willie Dodd had a scheme for a sort of syndicate to take it over. So, five of them bought the shares from the Misses Jonas.'

'How long have you been employed here, Mr. Bugler?'

'Fifteen years.'

He said it sadly, as though they were years the locusts had eaten.

'And you didn't become one of the directors at the takeover?'

Mr. Bugler showed signs of lively indignation.

'I wasn't asked, but I wouldn't have put a penny in it. Not with John Willie Dodd running the place.'

'You didn't like Dodd?'

'He was all right, but no good at bossing a firm like this. He was secretary when Mr. Jonas was alive. He didn't know anything about the practical side of the business. Thomas Hoop, the old man, was manager. He was good when he was in his prime, but he's eighty now and past it. The place has been going down ever since they took over from Mr. Jonas.'

'What did they pay for it?'

'Five thousand pounds. The Jonas family owned the freehold and the two daughters leased it to the new company at a rent. The five thousand the new directors scraped together went to buy the machinery, which was past its prime at the time. If it had been auctioned, it would have sold for scrap-iron. But Dodd persuaded the rest that there was a fortune in keeping the firm running. So, they went on and, judging from results, they've lost every penny they put in it.'

It was a dismal tale. Littlejohn looked round the dusty office and through the glass partition into the silent forlorn workshop. Failure and struggle all over it.

'The directors, then. Who were they?'

'Thomas Hoop was chairman and Fred, his son, was what they called managing director. Thomas was, as I said, manager for Mr. Jonas, and knew the business well. Fred was foreman in the machine shop, and the old man had forgotten more than Fred knew. It was a mistake giving Fred all that responsibility. He couldn't take it. John Willie Dodd stayed as secretary, but it was really him who ran the place. They were always up against finance. Not enough capital and Dodd did the scraping, borrowing, getting credit to keep the place alive. It was hopeless from the start. Richard Fallows was head of the joinery shop. He became a director, too. John Robert Piper was stock foreman. His wife had a bit of money, so he was made a director, also. He was a decent chap, but like a fish out of water on the board. That was the set-up.'

It all sounded depressing and the way Bugler described it, in his dull, flat voice, gave it an atmosphere of doom like that created by a Greek chorus.

'They didn't make a go of it, then?'

'At first things seemed good. They were running on Mr. Jonas's reputation and credit, then. But this business of what they call pre-pared joinery has got in the hands of big groups now, with modern machines. They soon knock a place like this for six. Couldn't hope to compete. Dodd cut prices below profit margins and, in the end, they had to take in loan monies from whoever they could persuade to lend them. Relatives mostly. Dodd could tell a good tale and, right to the end, seemed able to persuade people this was a little gold mine. Well, it's over now. Dodd, Fallows and Piper dead, and Mr. Thomas Hoop at death's door. I heard this morning that his 'flu had turned to pneumonia and his chances of recovery are very poor.'

Four out of five directors extinguished overnight! What a case! Through a dirty window which overlooked Green Lane and the timber-yard, Littlejohn could see a group of men, presumably the idle workers, gathered round the gatehouse, talking with the gatekeeper. Their faces were grave and they almost moved about on tiptoes. One of them was laying down the law, gesticulating, beating the palm of one hand with the back of the other. His talk and grievances didn't seem to be making much impression. The men were too stunned.

Mr. Oswald Bugler picked up a pile of bills and threw them back on the desk with a disgruntled gesture.

'Completely bust! That's what we are. Bust. And what next? Only one man left of the board and him a lightweight. I expect the next move'll be the bailiffs'll be in.'

Littlejohn glanced at Cromwell, who'd been very silent through it all. He was frowning and looking as if he were battling himself with the problem of extricating the sorry business from its troubles.

'What do you think, old man?'

Cromwell awoke from his reverie with a start.

'It beats me.'

He grinned.

'Did you ever see such a mess? If you read about a thing like this in a novel, you'd say it was a bit overdone, wouldn't you?'

Ossie, who had been rummaging among the piles of invoices and bills, as though, somewhere hidden among them, was the solution to the present disaster, suddenly straightened himself and, *á propos* of nothing, gave tongue.

'Excelsior Joinery Company! I seem to remember from a poem I used to recite at school, that Excelsior means up and up. What's the word for down and down...'

Littlejohn said that he couldn't give him the answer on the spur of the moment and Cromwell looked at Ossie as though he'd suddenly gone round the bend.

'The company was borrowing heavily from the bank, Mr. Bugler?'

Bugler shrugged.

'As heavily as Roper – that's the manager – would let 'em. And the overdraft was bigger than I'd care to lend. What was there to lend against? They don't own the property and the machinery's antiquated. Dodd, who could talk his way in or out of anything, persuaded Roper to lend them five thousand against the guarantee of all the directors and a charge over the machinery. They soon spent the whole lot... The whole five thousand, I mean. Dodd bought in timber and the rest went to keep the creditors quiet. Now that this has happened and the place will probably have to shut up, I don't see how Roper's going to get his money back. All the directors had was in the company. Their guarantee'll be worth damn' all, and as for the machinery... Well... It looks as if Roper's in for a bad debt.'

The sorry tale was interrupted by the arrival of Tattersall, ploughing through the mass of shavings on the floor outside, smiling as though his prosecution of the local toughs had been highly successful. He thrust his head round the door of the partition.

Bugler raised his baggy eyes.

'You've not come to tell us that Fred Hoop's hung himself? It only needs that to finish the lot.'

He wasn't joking and looked as if he'd been disappointed with anything short of an affirmative.

'No. I haven't heard of anything so bad, but Roper, the bank manager, is outside asking for Fred Hoop, and judging from the look in his eye, he's called to murder him.'

Bugler seemed determined to squeeze the last drop of misery from the situation. He cackled dismally.

'If Roper doesn't do him in, the workmen will, when it comes pay-day. There's not a cent in cash around the place for wages, and Roper's already said he won't provide the money. There'll be some more explosions round here on Friday.'

Outside the knots of men were breaking up. It was lunchtime and the man at the gatehouse was sharing his sandwiches with a stray dog.

3

LEGAL ADVICE

I T WAS THREE IN THE AFTERNOON. CROMWELL, WHO WAS never idle, was sitting in a room at the police station making his report.

Littlejohn was lolling opposite, smoking his pipe and reading the file on the case which Tattersall had handed to him. He looked at his watch.

'They're taking a long time finding Fred Hoop.'

Tattersall was in court again. He never seemed out of it. The justices of the peace appeared to be more intent on dealing with petty motor offences and in punishing hooligans than in finding the pyrotechnician of Green Lane.

Fred Hoop had been absent all morning. Some said he was consulting fire loss assessors; others that he'd done a bunk rather than face his angry unpaid workmen. Littlejohn was very anxious to see Fred. With the exception of his dying father, he was all that was left of the board of the expiring joinery company.

Cromwell looked up blankly. He'd been concentrating on his writing, living for a while in the town of Evingden.

Cromwell always made a few notes on the locality and scene of the crime. Evingden needed a bit of describing. Little more than a large village of 3,000 people ten years ago, it had been swollen by an overspill of another 15,000. A new town had been built beside the old one and a conglomeration of new shops and public buildings, most of them architectural monstrosities, with a sprawl of housing schemes surrounding them, had swamped a one-time pleasant locality.

Fred Hoop lived on the outskirts of the new town. After lunch, Littlejohn and Cromwell had called to see him and found the house empty.

It was a new, modern place, quite out of keeping with the penniless company of which Hoop was a director. Tattersall explained that Hoop's father-in-law had made him and his bride, Bella, a present of it on their marriage. A man called Sandman, who'd made a lot of money buying and selling government surplus after the war. Cromwell had described the house in his notes.

A large affair, with a green roof, lawns, flower-beds and two ancient carriage-lamps, electrically illuminated, one on each side of the front door. The house was called Bella Vista, which, after subsequent speculative builders had finished with the sites around it, sounded more ironical than real.

The Hoops were obviously having difficulty in keeping up the place. The buildings needed painting and pointing and the grounds were shabby. Mrs. Hoop was perhaps finding it hard to keep up the appearances of both her wedding present and her husband. Her father had died not long after giving her away in holy matrimony and left an estate of next to nothing. It was said that he had secretly given sums to his wife and daughter from untaxed profits in the scrap trade.

When Cromwell had looked through the closed green shutters from which the faded paint was peeling, he'd had a surprise. The rooms were almost bare. The sumptuous furniture with which Sandman had endowed the house was gone, along with the heavy carpets. It had, according to a nearby neighbour, been recently

removed in a plain van. This seemed to support the rumour that
Fred Hoop had fled to distant parts.

> *Bought on H.P.? Re-possessed?*
> *Sold to keep up appearances?*
> *Sold to finance business?*
> *Sold preparatory to flight?*

Cromwell had made notes with question marks in the margin of
his report to show how his mind was working.

That was as far as he had got when heavy feet outside announced
the arrival of visitors. It was Fred Hoop himself, accompanied by
two constables from a police car. He looked as if they'd arrested
him for murder, arson, larceny and a lot of other things.

'We found him on a bike, sir, cycling in the direction of
Brantwood,' explained one of the bobbies, who was panting,
either from enthusiasm or after a struggle with Fred.

Fred wasn't going to take it lying down. His collar and tie were
dishevelled, his hair was windblown from his athletic efforts, and
his suit looked to have been slept in the night before, but he still
retained his fighting dignity.

'And why shouldn't I go to Brantwood on my bike, if I like?
My mother-in-law lives there and my wife's been staying with her.
After the commotion of yesterday, she's on the edge of a nervous
breakdown. There were newspaper reporters camping in our
garden overnight. It's a disgrace… And to cap the lot, these chaps
started chasing me along the road and insisted on bringing me in.
You might think it was me who blew up the works. I shan't do
anything or say anything without my lawyer…'

And he sank exhausted in a chair in the corner.

Littlejohn looked at him blandly.

'We're not accusing you of anything, sir. We're here to give you all the help we can. After last night's disaster, you're the only remaining director of the company in circulation. We need some assistance from you and we've been hunting all over the place for you. Where have you been?'

'That's my business. I wasn't bolting with the rest of the firm's resources, if that's what you're hinting. Business has to be carried on in spite of what happened last night. I've been chasing here, there and everywhere with that in mind.'

Actually, Fred had been doing a round of banks, insurance companies and other sources of finance trying to raise the wind to pay his workmen's wages. He didn't know that Littlejohn had heard about it all and he wasn't going to tell him.

Cromwell looked up from his notes.

'Have you been selling your house, Mr. Hoop?'

"That's a silly question. Why should I sell my house? Do you think I've gone up the wall?'

'It's empty. The furniture's all gone.'

'And what's that to do with you? It has nothing to do with last night's affair...'

Cromwell looked at his list of enquiries and wondered whether or not to reel them off. Re-possessed by H.P. firm; sold? In any case he didn't get a chance. More pattering feet and the door opened. A constable ushered in a stranger. A youngish man of around forty, dressed in a black jacket, and grey striped trousers, with a small moustache and curly black hair. Not a hair out of place, either, and his linen was white and clean. His dark eyes were sparkling with eagerness.

'Mister Hash!' announced the conducting bobby.

The newcomer didn't wait for introductions. First he made a correction.

'Ash, without the aitch, if you please.'

Then he addressed Littlejohn.

'Good afternoon, Superintendent. I presume you are Littlejohn. And this is Inspector Cromwell. I've heard about you both and I'm glad to meet you both. I'm Mr. Fred Hoop's solicitor...'

He turned to Hoop, who, fortified by his presence, now gave him a watery smile.

'I'm sorry to be late, Fred. I was in court...'

Then he turned to Littlejohn again. The fellow was like one of the figures in a Punch and Judy show. Agitated with energy; addressing first one side of the stage and then the other; shrugging and gesticulating.

'Mr. Hoop telephoned my office for me. As I said, I was out. In court. First of all, I must ask you to excuse Mr. Hoop's rather strange conduct in absenting himself from the enquiry. After all, he had his men's wages to attend to. Very commendable in the middle of other troubles. Men must live and eat and without wages... Well... Besides, the trade union secretary was on the doorstep at crack o' dawn about it... So, you see...'

Littlejohn was fascinated by the little lawyer. He seemed possessed of an athlete's second wind, and went on talking long after his breath should have failed. The magistrates must have been terrified of him.

'...feel I must tell you right away that Mr. Hoop has sent for me more as a friend than as his solicitor. He in no way wishes to obstruct your enquiries. As a matter of fact, he wishes to co-operate to the utmost. The deaths of his co-directors and the serious state of his father's health, however, have confused him somewhat, and, as he isn't very familiar with police methods... Well... You understand?'

'Of course, sir.'

'I'm glad you do. I'll do my best to make matters easy for you. Please don't regard me as defending my client. I'll just sit in at the interrogation and let you get on with it.'

Littlejohn sighed with relief. Fred Hoop emerged from his corner, dragging his chair behind him and sat near Littlejohn, as though assured by his lawyer that the Superintendent was perfectly harmless and could be patted on the head, like a good dog.

Littlejohn set about him right away, before Mr. Ash started again.

'Have you any idea what might have caused last night's explosion and fire, Mr. Hoop?'

'No, I haven't. I wish I had.'

'You know, don't you, that it seems to have been deliberately done and that blasting powder was used?'

'That's what the police say. I haven't any idea why anybody should want to blow the place up. As for blasting powder, well... it beats me. We didn't keep any in the office... Or anywhere else for that matter. What would we want with blasting powder? It's a joiners' shop, not a quarry or a battleship.'

He looked around at everybody, especially in the direction of Mr. Ash, waiting for an answer. Mr. Ash nodded, as though approving of the rhetorical question.

'It seems very strange to me too, Mr. Hoop. Supposing someone... I say, just supposing. I'm making no insinuations. Supposing someone wished to set fire to the place and collect the insurance...'

Fred Hoop leapt to his feet, livid, and began to thrash about with his arms.

'I've heard that said several times before this mornin'. It's been insinuated that *I've* done it. Well... It's a damned lie. I never...'

Mr. Ash raised a languid, well-manicured hand in the direction of Fred.

'Don't get so upset, Fred. The Superintendent emphasised that he was making no insinuations. Let him ask his questions. If any question or answer isn't fair or permissible, I'll tell you. That's what I'm here for.'

Hoop ceased to effervesce and cast a grateful look upon his lawyer.

'Thanks, Hartley. I appreciate that.'

He turned to Littlejohn.

'Go on, then.'

'I was merely making a comment, not an accusation. I was going to say that, even if someone had arson in mind, either for insurance purposes or even for revenge or spite, they'd hardly have blown the place up with dynamite. And why the office, which is a minor part of the company's buildings and containing nothing, presumably, but records and a few items of furniture? They'd have set fire to the main buildings or the timber-yard.'

'A good point,' said Mr. Hartley Ash to Fred.

'We're therefore inclining to the idea that there was something personal about it. In other words, whoever committed the crime was intent on blowing up... or, to put it more plainly, murdering one or all of the occupants of the office.'

Fred Hoop's jaw dropped.

'Murder? That's ridiculous. Who'd want to murder Dick Fallows, Jack Piper or John Willie Dodd...?'

Old Uncle Tom Cobley and all, thought Cromwell to himself.

'I don't know. That's what we've got to find out. What were they doing there at that time, sir?'

Fred Hoop looked nettled. He was supposed to know all the answers about Excelsior Joinery affairs, but this one beat him.

'I don't know,' he said vaguely, trying to pass it off. 'Dodd must have asked them to meet him about something. Perhaps a problem had cropped up about an order or the work in the factory. In any case, it wasn't an official directors' meeting. If it had been, Bugler would have been there taking the minutes. Lucky for him, it wasn't. In any case, I'd have had to be there. I'm vice-chairman, you see, and with my father being ill, I'd have had to take the chair.'

'To your knowledge, Mr. Hoop, had any of the dead men enemies, or had they been threatened at all recently, in any way whatever?'

'Certainly not.'

'I suppose you'd know if they had?'

'Of course I would. They were friends, co-directors, always about the place. I know all that goes on at the factory. I'd have got to know if there'd been anything like that.'

Littlejohn wondered. Hoop wasn't the sort he'd care to confide in, whatever anybody else's inclination might be. Too cocky, excitable and a bit stupid.

'The relations between all the directors were amicable?'

'Certainly. Why not?'

'Hasn't the company been having financial troubles, sir? If that's the case, it might have stirred up an atmosphere of irritability, perhaps even recrimination.'

'Who's been talking? Who's been casting reflections on the credit and solvency of the firm?'

Hoop looked in the direction of Mr. Hartley Ash as though wondering whether or not to commence suit for slander. Mr. Ash thought that perhaps he ought to say something.

'Excuse me interrupting, Superintendent, but have you any specific information about the financial state of Excelsior Joinery Company. If so, I'd like to know the source of it, although you'll probably refuse to divulge it...'

'You know as well as I do, sir, that it's known all over the town. When you have a bunch of workmen wondering where their past week's wages are coming from, you can hardly expect talk about the company's solvency not to circulate.'

'Thank you. Go on.'

'I believe that, although he was officially secretary, John Willie Dodd had a major share in the direction and administration of the firm.'

'You seem to know a lot considering you've only been here a few hours. I'm managing director, and the policy of the company rests with me, subject to the overall approval of the board of directors.'

Hoop closed his eyes and puffed out his chest a bit, trying to convince them all of his status and authority.

'Didn't Dodd, however, travel about, booking orders, buying timber, generally representing the company to outsiders? You, sir, I take it, had charge of the manufacturing side.'

Hoop looked happier now. This was, to him, a very satisfactory compromise, which maintained his dignity.

'That's right.'

Outside, the business of the court was going on. Figures kept passing the windows on their ways to and from the bench. You could almost give them a label. Erring motorists, deflated hooligans, victims of matrimonial quarrels, including a man with a black eye, surrounded by what appeared to be all his relatives...

'Who looked after the finances?'

'The board. What's that got to do with the case?'

'Perhaps quite a lot.'

Mr. Ash nodded, but in a fashion which indicated that Littlejohn had better mind his Ps and Qs.

'Well, the board was responsible for that.'

'Who was their spokesman, say, in banking matters?'

Mr. Hartley Ash jerked his head suddenly. Ready to pounce on Littlejohn if he went too far.

'The secretary, of course. Who else?'

'Were you overdrawn at the bank?'

Littlejohn paused for Mr. Ash's protest. It came.

'You have no authority to ask that question, Superintendent. I recommend my client not to answer. It is quite irrelevant.'

'I can find out, sir.'

'Not without an order from the court, which will, in the present circumstances, be difficult to obtain.'

'Then let me answer the question myself, sir. There *is* an over-draft, it has reached the limit of arrangements and the bank is not prepared to grant any more.'

'I can see, Superintendent, you have been talking with someone who's been indiscreet. I shall have to...'

'Mr. Ash. The indiscretion seems to have been committed by the directors themselves. Even their workmen in the street can tell you that there's an overdraft, that the company depends on the bank for its continuance, and that the directors have been asking for more. Some can even tell you how much they owe.'

'Why, then, did you ask my client the question?'

'I thought it would be more seemly for him to tell me, instead of me to tell him. However, that didn't seem to be the way he wanted it.'

Mr. Hartley Ash yawned.

'Will you wish to interview my client much longer, Superintendent? I've another case in court and I'll have to be leaving you very soon.'

Fred Hoop began to lose confidence.

'I'm not saying else else if you're not here, Hartley. I said so before you came and I'm saying it again.'

Littlejohn kept his patience by taking out his pouch and slowly filling his pipe.

'You talk as if we were accusing you of a crime, Mr. Hoop, instead of seeking your co-operation in a case which very much concerns you. I suggest before Mr. Ash leaves us, you tell me something about your co-directors of the firm and how they came to own the place.'

'I've about ten minutes, and then I must go,' said Mr. Ash wearily, as though, without some warning, Hoop would talk for the rest of the day and far into the night.

'What did you want to know?'

'There are... or were... five directors. How did you come by the company?'

Littlejohn opened the file which Tattersall had given him. Most of it was there, but Littlejohn wished to hear it all again. He wanted Hoop's own tale.

'It was a family business before we took over. Henry Jonas and Son. There seems to have been about four Henrys, father and son, ever since it started. The last Mr. Henry dropped dead in the works nearly six years since. He'd no sons and his two daughters wanted to sell the business. Five of us clubbed together and bought it. It had been a very profitable firm... a money-spinner... in its day, but we found out after we bought it that it had been run down and made very small profits for a few years. The accountant who sold it

to us for the Misses Jonas, diddled us... It was a swindle. He knew
that without a Jonas in the company a lot of the goodwill would
go. We began to make losses from the start. We all put our backs
in it, but we'd bitten off more than we could chew...'

Littlejohn liked Mr. Hoop's metaphors and the way he tried to
make out that what seemed to be obvious incompetence in running the firm was really due to a swindle in the accounts when
they'd taken over.

Mr. Hartley Ash was sighing and looking at his watch again. No
use going through the rigmarole which Bugler had already given
and suffering from Fred Hoop's bitter commentaries.

'How old was Dodd?'

'Eh?'

Fred's line of thought had suddenly been switched and he had
to readjust himself.

'How old was Dodd?'

'About fifty-five. If you want the ages of the rest – and I can't
see what good it'll do you – if you want the ages you can have
them. My father's seventy-nine; and Fallows was nearly seventy.
Is that all?'

'Had they any families employed in the works?'

'No. I've a brother in Canada and a sister married and living
in London. Piper had a son killed in the war and a daughter and
Fallows had no children. Are you satisfied?'

'Thank you. Now if I return to finance, don't go up in the air,
Mr. Hoop. I merely ask as it may be important in this case.'

Hoop gave him a guarded, almost challenging look and Mr.
Ash began to sit up and take notice again.

'I told you before, I know that you depended on the bank for
running capital to finance the business. As for buying the company

from the Jonas family, you all subscribed to a pool from which the firm was purchased. Right?'

'Of course it's right. How else could we do it?'

'The money came from your own funds? Savings and so on? Were there any other shareholders?'

'Answer, Fred. No harm in it.'

Had Mr. Ash not butted in with advice, Hoop might have resisted.

'The directors found the bulk of the money. Their wives found a bit, too, and received shares for it.'

'When the bank refused to find more money, you had to find it yourselves, I presume.'

'Yes. We and a few friends collected some loan money. We ought to have gone into liquidation then, instead of throwing good money after bad, but Dodd was so persuasive. He said we'd turned the corner and would soon be making good profits. He fooled us. The loan money went the way of the rest. Now we're in Queer Street good and proper, as you seem to be well aware.'

'Did Dodd have a good share in the company?'

'No, he didn't. Of the cash subscribed, Dodd provided about one tenth. He'd no money of his own. He'd always lived extravagantly and he borrowed his share from his wife's mother. We ought never to have allowed him in with us and certainly not given him his head the way we did. But he'd been Mr. Henry Jonas's right-hand man, knew all the customers, knew the timber trade, and was well up in the accounts and such like. We couldn't do without him at the time, so we let him in cheap.'

Mr. Ash rose to his feet with a bored expression.

'I must be going.'

Littlejohn got in a farewell question.

'When Mr. Ash came in, Mr. Hoop, you were discussing with Inspector Cromwell why your house was almost empty of furniture…'

'Discussin'…? I like that. He was trying to browbeat me into telling him why I've sent the best of my furniture to my mother-in-law's at Brantwood. Well, I don't feel compelled to answer the question. It's not relevant in this case.'

Mr. Ash's sallow face became suffused with blood.

'You mean to say that you moved it in spite of my advice. I feel like letting you stew in your own juice, Hoop. It was a very silly thing to do. A futile move. The furniture is your wife's. Her father gave it to her. If the bank call up your guarantee and take you to court because you can't find the money, they can on no account seize either your house or your furniture, simply because it's *not* yours. *It's your wife's.* You've moved all the furniture for nothing.'

'I moved it because I once knew a man who was in a similar fix. The bank took all his goods. Every bloomin' one. Including the bed. Turned him in the street…'

'Rubbish! In the first place, no bank would do such a thing. For a few sticks of furniture they wouldn't make their reputation stink before the public… They just wouldn't do it, even if they could.'

'Well, I know better. And while you're at it, my furniture isn't just a few sticks. It's worth hundreds of pounds…'

It was Littlejohn's turn this time to tell the rest he must be going and he gathered up Cromwell, the files and their other belongings and left Hoop and Ash quarrelling furiously about points of law and other more personal matters.

4

THE GATEKEEPER

T HE LONG NEW HIGH STREET OF THE NEW TOWN OF EVINGDEN was brightly illuminated by modern flashy pale-blue tubes, but these did not spread very far. The lighting system deteriorated as the distance from the town hall increased and by the time it reached Green Lane, it was reduced to old gas lamps. The latter were a kind of ancient monument, surviving in memory of Alderman Maypole, former mayor and chairman of the local gas board. After the glare of the satellite part of the town, the lamps of the suburbs seemed to shed a soft pale-green light over the silent street and its old houses.

The way back to London passed near Green Lane and Littlejohn made a diversion to see what the place looked like after dark. It was deadly quiet. Lights shone behind the damaged windows, but there wasn't a soul moving. It was as if they were all expecting another explosion at any time. In fact, someone had thought out and circulated an alarming theory that there was a sort of Jack the Ripper around, using sticks of dynamite instead of a knife. On the strength of this tale, two spinsters who lived alone and a man who believed in taking no risks had gone to stay with relatives under the bright lights of the new town housing estates.

One solitary electric light was visible shining over the Excelsior timber-yard. The whole of this large storage area was surrounded by a wall, built years ago when such erections were much cheaper. The top of the wall was covered by cement sown with broken bottles and further fortified by a cage of rusty barbed wire. The only entrance was in Green Lane, a large wooden gate, guarded by a gatehouse.

The man inside the gatehouse was normally a little cheerful chap, but now he was very worried. He greeted Littlejohn and Cromwell very civilly and almost at once began to confide his troubles to Littlejohn.

'Have you any idea what's goin' to happen to the Excelsior when all this is over? Are they goin' to carry on or will they go bust and the whole show come under the 'ammer?'

His visitors might have been a couple of accountants or fortune-tellers instead of detectives.

The gatekeeper, whose name was Wood, then seemed to realise that it wasn't good manners to discuss his problems with two strangers until the formalities of introductions had been gone through.

'Are you two gentlemen the auditors come to see what's been happenin' lately with the firm?'

'No. We're detectives investigating last night's catastrophe. I'm Superintendent Littlejohn and this is Inspector Cromwell.'

There was a small table nearby at which the little man had been busy when they entered. It was laid with a large teapot, a plate on which stood a soggy steak pudding from a tin, and half a loaf with a large piece of butter on a wax paper beside it.

'My name's Wood. Augustus Wood, but they call me Joe,' said the keeper of the gate, and he took two large mugs from a cupboard on the wall and laid them beside his own on the table. He added milk from a bottle and sugar from a blue paper packet and filled up all three with the brackish-looking liquid from the pot before he spoke again.

'Tea? I'm just having mine, so you might as well have a cup with me. Sit down.'

He indicated two tall wooden stools, presumably throw-outs from the main office, and handed over the mugs. Then he tackled his tinned pudding.

'Excuse me if I get on with me tea. It's gettin' cold.'

He filled his mouth with food and masticated it with vigorous relish. 'What did you want at this time o' day?'

He wore an old suit a size too large for him which gave him a wilting appearance. His cloth cap might have been a part of his head for he never moved it. In place of his left hand he had a hook, with which he manipulated his tea-things with great skill. Obviously another casualty of the woodwork machinery trade who had been given a lighter job after his accident. He must have been past sixty and, in spite of his ill-lighted and confined job, had managed to keep a chubby cheerful countenance.

'We were passing and thought we'd pay a call on you. You must see most that goes on around this place.'

'You bet I do.'

He thoughtfully cut a thick slice from his loaf and plastered it copiously with butter. Then he took a large bite of it. 'I've been on the job for twenty years, ever since my accident, and there isn't much happens that I don't know of.'

He showed them his hook, as though it were some strange appendage he'd grown himself.

There must have been a loft above the room for they could hear scratching noises, as though it might be infested with rats. And yet rats didn't make the sounds going on up there. Noises between a purr and a coo. Mr. Wood must have seen Littlejohn's glance at the ceiling.

'Them's my pigeons. I'm a pigeon-flyer in my spare time. Homin'. Won a lot of prizes and cups with 'em. That's wot's worryin' me. If this place shuts up, wot's goin' to happen to me and my birds?'

'You don't live here, do you, Mr. Wood?'

'No; I'm a widower with a little house of my own, but I spend most of my time here, because of the pigeons. With them around, it feels like home.'

'You don't act as night-watchman?'

'No. I generally go home around eight o'clock. Then the place is locked up. There's not much anybody would want to steal here. Logs of wood and planks is too heavy to run off with and not be found out.'

'Were you here when the explosion occurred?'

'Yes. I wondered what the 'ell was up. It shook the whole neighbourhood. You could hear the stock of timber near the office tumblin' about as if somebody was chucking it all over the place. I was near the window and the bang seemed to blow all the office windows out and the place was blazin' before you could say knife. I rushed out to the nearest 'phone, which is in Mr. Bugler's office in the works, the one in the main offices, of course, bein' impossible to get at. I called up the fire brigade and then ran back to the fire. There wasn't a thing anybody could do till the brigade got here. It was burnin' like hell by then.'

'What time did this happen?'

'I'd just looked at the clock before the explosion. It was on five minutes to eight. And it's five minutes slow.'

'Did you see anybody about when you ran to the telephone?'

'No. I was so put out by what had 'appened and in such a hurry to get the fire engine that I didn't see anythin' else. I had a key to the workshop. They gave me one years since. I come here every day to attend to me birds and when holidays are on and at week-ends, they like me to take a look over the works, like, and to see that all's well. Lucky I had a key...'

He contemplatively mopped up the remains of his steak pudding, drank the rest of his tea, and wiped his solitary hand down his trousers.

'More tea?'

'No, thanks.'

He collected the crockery and put it on a table in the corner for washing-up. Then he pulled out a short pipe and lit it.

'Did you know the directors well?'

'Yes. Known 'em all their lives. I was here as a woodwork machineman till my accident. Then, after I'd got over it, Mr. Jonas gave me this job. Tom Hoop, the old man, that is, was 'ere as foreman when I started. Fred Hoop was quite a nipper then and was taken on later as apprentice. Piper and Fallows were journeymen joiners, too. John Willie Dodd... I remember him comin' as clerk in the office and then he rose to be secretary of the company, which he was when Mr. Jonas died and the firm changed hands.'

'It didn't change for the better, I hear.'

'That's right. It didn't. It was what you'd call a matter of class. Although his grandfather, who started the place, had risen from bein' a journeyman carpenter, Mr. Henry Jonas, his grandson, was a real gentleman. He'd been educated proper and he'd got that kindness and consideration for his workmen that you don't often find these days. He could also talk as an equal, man to man, to merchants, the bank, the people at the town hall and such like. The directors who followed him were decent chaps, but they hadn't got the right approach, if you get what I mean...'

'I do.'

'…They were either too aggressive or too shy. No 'appy medium. The 'appy medium goes a long way in business. Easy does it. Neither a bully nor a toady. Just easy's the way.'

Mr. Wood then knocked out the dottle of his pipe and began to cut a fresh fill from a piece of thick twist. He gently rubbed the tobacco between his one hand and the table top, skilfully inserted it in his pipe, struck a match with one hand, and lit the result.

'You're quite a psychologist, Mr. Wood.'

'I've an idea what you mean, sir. I used to be a football referee in my younger days. Nothin' like a bit of refereein' to get to know yewman nature. If you can 'andle twenty-two footballers in front of a crowd of thousands, you can 'andle anybody.'

'What did you think of Dodd?'

Mr. Wood looked around the place as though expecting listeners in the shadows.

'Not much.'

'Why?'

Another cautious look around. He puffed his pipe until his head was almost lost in a fog of smoke.

'Bit of an upstart. Look 'ere. A man oughtn't to speak ill of the dead, but this death isn't the usual sort. If I express myself truthfully, you'll see it doesn't get out of these four walls?'

'We'll regard it as confidential.'

'Well, I consider the way this firm's gone downhill as due to Dodd. The other directors was putty in 'is hands. He'd got the gift of the gab. Could persuade you that black was white if you didn't look out. The other directors was just plain workmen. What did they know about business and 'igh finance? Not a thing. Give 'em tools and some timber and they could do a first class job o' joinery. But tell 'em to find money to run the business or get orders and sell wot they made and they were completely at sea. They left that part to Dodd, who never stopped blowin' his own trumpet. When, at the end of the year, he told them they'd made a loss, they didn't know why. They just left it to Dodd. Till, in the end, they couldn't do without 'im. Even if they wanted to sack 'im, they daren't 'ave, because it would bring down the whole firm. Get me?'

'Yes.'

'They'd many a reason for wantin' to get rid of him, believe me. I don't go around with me eyes closed. I could tell you a thing or two...'

He loosened the tobacco in the bowl of his pipe with the hook on his left arm and lit up again.

'Tell us a thing or two then, Mr. Wood.'

Joe Wood evidently though the policemen were still under the oath of secrecy and he went ahead without more ado.

'Dodd has risen from nothin', as I said before. He started as a junior clerk and got on a lot by his wits. He was a good talker, too, and could talk his way in and out of anythin'...'

In the loft above the movements continued and one of the birds would begin to make soothing noises, as though comforting the rest.

Outside, there was dead silence. Now and then footsteps in the street or the backfiring of a passing car. Through the window they could see the glow in the sky caused by the gaudy lighting of the new town up the hill.

'As Dodd got on, his ideas got bigger. He even took a fancy to Mr. Jonas's youngest daughter, Miss Eva, but Miss Eva had her feet on the ground. Besides, she was a lot older than Dodd. She soon choked him off. Dodd was always a fancy man and one for the ladies. He was after money if he married, but ended by puttin' a plumber's daughter in the family way. He'd likely as not have dodged marryin' her, but she happened to have a very determined father and two brothers, strappin' chaps who stood no nonsense. They saw to it that he made an 'onest woman of her.'

Joe Wood smiled maliciously to himself, enjoying the passing thought of certain incidents in the love-life and shotgun wedding of John Willie Dodd.

'Dodd was a Yorkshireman and his wife's brothers soon taught 'im that Surrey men could show their teeth just as well as he could. Since then, Dodd 'asn't been satisfied with his own wife, although they've a couple of nice kids. Always some other woman in tow. Married or single, it was all the same to Dodd. His latest was Fred Hoop's missus. What they saw in him, I don't know, but they didn't seem able to resist him...'

'What sort of fellow was he?'

Joe Wood opened a drawer of the table on which he ate his meals and produced some postcard photographs.

'These are photos of the annual shop-trip, the outin' to the seaside that Excelsior had every year. It was started by Mr. Henry Jonas, who used to pay all expenses. After he died, we carried on, but we paid our own.'

Wood selected the best picture and with his hook pointed out various members of the group arranged in a semi-circle, dressed in their best and looking very merry.

'That's me...'

He was dressed in his Sunday suit and smoking his pipe.

'Them's Fallows and Piper...'

They were sitting on the front row with most of the rest standing behind. The directors, presumably, were allotted the places of honour, like heavenly bodies with satellites revolving round them.

Fallows and Piper were a couple of nondescript little men, the sort you wouldn't take a second look at if you passed them in the street. Honest to goodness workmen who'd suddenly found themselves elevated to doubtful headships in the fading Excelsior.

In the very centre of the group sat three dominant figures. Fred Hoop they knew. There he was, self-conscious and aggressive as ever, a cigarette stuck in the corner of his mouth, his thumbs in the armholes of his waistcoat, in what he thought was a nonchalant pose, his legs crossed and a portion of one bare calf showing above his sock. Very different from the man on his right.

'That's old Tom Hoop...'

Old Tom. The name seemed to suit him. The patriarch. A stern-looking man with a large white moustache. He wore a black soft hat, a dark suit, with a watch-chain across his middle. He was glaring at the photographer as though he'd been dragged in against his will.

'John Willie Dodd...'

They might have guessed. The dandy of the lot. The masher and lady-killer. He wore a light grey suit and a soft hat at a rakish angle. He was smoking a cigar.

'It's a good one of him. Taken last summer. You wouldn't think the business was on the rocks, would you? You'd think he'd struck oil proper, eh?'

Which was true. Sitting at the right hand of the chairman of Excelsior in his light grey suit Dodd looked like the *éminence grise* of the company, the one who ran the lot, however badly. Littlejohn examined Dodd through his pocket-glass.

Under the jaunty hat was a broad forehead tapering down to a small, firm chin. The nose was heavy and turned up a bit, like a snout, displaying the wide nostrils. In the photograph, the eyes looked dead, protruding from wrinkled baggy sockets, as though Dodd were sneering at the antics of the man with the camera.

'Was he florid or pale…?'

'Oh, florid, if by that you mean red. He was fond of his whisky and high life. When all the rest of us was waitin' for our wages, which were hard to come by sometimes if the bank got sticky… I say, if we was waitin', he always seemed to have enough. I guess he always saw that he got the first cut. Him and his family lived well, I can tell you.'

'Was he tall?'

'Medium… About five foot ten, I'd say. Well-built…'

As far as possible, Littlejohn had now an idea of what the main actors, particularly Dodd, looked like. Beyond that, he knew little as yet.

'You were saying he fancied Fred Hoop's wife?'

Wood lit his pipe again and nodded.

'She's a bit past her best now, but in her prime, she was a smasher, if you like 'em that way. A red-head and always ready for a bit o' fun. She came from nothin'. Her father was a scrap-iron merchant who did well in the war and after, sellin' surplus. He didn't leave much in his will when he died, but he must have salted a lot away. At any rate, Bella and Fred Hoop have gone short o' nothing durin' the bad times of the Excelsior. And I hear they've taken care that none of Bella's money's been put in the company.'

'And she and Dodd were having an affair?'

Wood removed his pipe and looked a bit startled. He was a man who came gently to things in diplomatic language.

'I didn't say so. I said they was sweet on one another.'

'What's the difference?'

Joe pondered on the niceties of expression.

'Let's put it this way. Between here and Brighton there's what they call a roadhouse, the Peepin' Tom. Why, I don't know, but it is. Now John Willie Dodd and Bella Hoop have been seen there havin' a meal together. That's what I'd call bein' sweet. If, on the other hand, somebody'd seen 'em goin' into or comin' out of one of the bedrooms, that would 'ave been what you call an affair. We call it carryin' on.'

'I see.'

'Did Fred Hoop know?'

'Like 'ell he did! If he hadn't, somebody would have seen he got to know. Him and Dodd had a flamin' row. But what was the good? If Dodd had packed up, as I said, the Excelsior would 'ave folded-up, too. He'd got Hoop and the rest of 'em where he wanted them.'

'And, also, if one of the directors, including the Hoops, had blown Dodd sky-high with a stick of blasting powder, they'd still have left the firm without a pilot?'

Joe Wood scratched his head through his cap.

'Yes. That's right. They would. But you can drive a man so far and no further. I'm not sayin' Fred Hoop had anything to do with what happened at the office, but suppose he felt he'd been made a fool of long enough. He's said to be fond of his missus, and I can quite believe it. They've got no kids and she's the boss of the pair. Suppose he'd had enough of Dodd makin' up to Bella. Fred Hoop's not the sort to give anybody else a good hidin' and be done with it. He's a bit of a rabbit, scared to death of force. I've seen that a time or two when he's had rows with the workmen about one thing or another. Any sign of fight and Fred's caved in. No; he's not the sort to have a scrap with Dodd about Bella. He might, in 'ot blood, let's say, shoot him...'

'Or throw a stick of dynamite at him?'

'If a stick of dynamite was to 'and when he lost his temper, yes.'

'But, as far as we can see, there wasn't a stick of dynamite handy...'

Wood looked stumped.

'There wasn't, was there? No, there wasn't.'

He seemed crestfallen that his theory had come to nothing.

'Could it have been any of the workmen? One with a grudge against Dodd; someone he'd sacked or offended...?'

'Not likely. I can't think of anybody who'd do a thing like that. If there's trouble in the shop, and they can't settle it on the floor level, they bring in the Union. Wilfred Julier's the local secretary. What Wilfred can't settle, isn't worth settlin'. No need for sticks of dynamite where he's concerned. He's dynamite himself.'

Now and then, in the course of the conversation, a head would be thrust round the door, and invariably withdrawn. This place seemed like a club, a place where men gathered in the evenings and gossiped together. As each newcomer appeared, Joe Wood seemed to give a signal that something private was going on and the intruder withdrew.

'What's the general opinion about the explosion, Joe?'

'The men seem as puzzled as you appear to be. It's one thing to give an unpopular chap a punch on the jaw, and quite another to chuck a stick of explosive at him. The best idea I heard was that there was somethin' in the coal...'

'Coal?'

'Yes, coal. There's been a bit of coal stealin' round here and a chap called Kelly had the idea of drillin' a hole in some pieces of coal and putting gunpowder in it. Not long after, a fireplace in one of the shady quarters of the town was blown out. Of course, Kelly couldn't prove a thing. It was a daft idea from the start. The damage was so bad, although nobody was 'urt, that Kelly daren't speak up. He told me in confidence here, one night, what he'd done. Thought it was clever. I told 'im he'd soon see how clever it was if somebody got killed. He'd be for the 'igh jump. Somebody suggested that one of Kelly's lumps of coal might have found its way into the office fire.'

'Dodd had been pinching coal?'

'I wouldn't put it past 'im, though he'd never go rootin' in the coal-sheds. Cookin' the books, perhaps, but nothing to soil his 'ands on.'

Wood began to gather his things together. It was time to go home. To say good night to the pigeons up aloft and then be off back to his silent house, which he kept as spick and span as it had been in his wife's days.

Littlejohn and Cromwell bade him good night and stepped out into the rain again.

There was nobody about. The gas-lamps were on and the rain surrounded each of them with a nimbus of small drops. The Excelsior works, all old brick punctuated with large windows which needed cleaning badly, reared itself above the neighbourhood like a huge shadow.

As Littlejohn and Cromwell reached the car a nearby door opened and emitted a shaft of light. Someone was putting out the cat for the night.

5

DYNAMITE

'I STILL THINK FRED HOOP'S THE ONE WE OUGHT TO WATCH...' Inspector Tattersall confided this to his local Superintendent to whom he conscientiously reported every step of the Excelsior enquiry. That was what it was labelled in the files: *Excelsior Joinery Case.* As though it involved petty larceny or book-cooking instead of three men being blown to Kingdom Come.

Tattersall hadn't a grain of malice or jealousy in his make-up, but he still thought that Littlejohn wasn't giving Fred Hoop enough attention. To make up for this neglect, he secretly put a detective constable on Fred's tail and had him followed all over the place.

Fred Hoop had once travelled around in an expensive car, financed, it was said, by his wife. Now, however, as though to show the creditors of the Excelsior that he was doing his best for them, he'd taken to a bicycle. This was very embarrassing for Longman, his shadow. He couldn't keep up with Fred on foot and a police car travelling at bicycle speed was ridiculous. So, Longman had to take to a bike himself and indulge in a furtive *Tour de France* after Fred. Naturally, it ended in Fred spotting his pursuer and complaining. His complaint was conveyed to the police by Mr. Boycott, the senior lawyer of the town.

Whatever had been said by Mr. Hartley Ash to Fred Hoop and by Fred to Hartley after Littlejohn left them in the little room at the police station, was never known, but it had obviously ended in a row, for Fred Hoop changed his lawyer after it and turned to his father's solicitor for guidance. Mr. Boycott therefore appeared in the little room allotted to Scotland Yard to present his protest. He was small, grey and talkative. He reminded Littlejohn very much of Herbert Rowse Armstrong, another solicitor of greater fame, who had poisoned his wife in 1921, and been hanged for it.

Whatever Littlejohn thought of *him*, Mr. Boycott seemed to think well of Littlejohn. He took a fancy to him right away. He shook hands and spoke in a piping voice.

'I'm ready to give you any information you may need which I think can reasonably be divulged. Contrary to what you might think, my client doesn't wish to hold anything back from the police. He wishes to co-operate. His conscience is quite clear. Ask me any question you like, but first please answer one for me. Why are you having my client followed all over the place? He's quite innocent of crime and is hardly likely to decamp.'

Whatever Fred Hoop was, his lawyers, Ash and Boycott, were a couple of ingratiating fellows!

'I'm afraid it was a bit of undue enthusiasm on the part of the local police. Naturally, from the little they know, Mr. Fred Hoop hasn't gone unsuspected. They wished to make sure he didn't disappear again when he was needed for questioning.'

'Disappear? I've heard nothing of his disappearing.'

'At a time when it was most important that we should have all available information and help, Mr. Hoop showed an inclination to take long bicycle rides in the country...'

'He was merely visiting his wife who's living at her mother's place in Brantwood for the present. He didn't wish to be seen driving about in a large car when his company was said to be in financial difficulties. That was all.'

'I've heard that since.'

'You mention his being suspect. Why?'

Mr. Boycott drew out a large handkerchief and trumpeted in it, polished his moustache vigorously, and restored the handkerchief deep into an inside pocket.

'There have been various theories as to why the offices were blown up. It might have been vandals. It could hardly have been safe-breakers operating with three directors in the room occupied by the safe. There was, therefore, an idea that it might have been an act of revenge. Dodd seems to have been having an affair with Mrs. Fred Hoop.'

'So Fred threw a stick of dynamite, or whatever it was…'

'It was, I've now heard from our experts, dynamite. Blasting sticks.'

'So, Fred, knowing, I presume, that Dodd wasn't alone, but in company of what might be called old friends of the Hoop family, threw a stick of explosive in the midst of them. Ridiculous! You'll have to do better than that, Superintendent.'

'As I said, sir, the local police got a bit too enthusiastic about the theory. I'm sorry if Mr. Fred Hoop has been embarrassed.'

'Let's forget it, then. Is there anything else?'

'Are you solicitor to the Excelsior Joinery Company, sir?'

'Yes. Why?'

'I gather they're in a bad way financially.'

Mr. Boycott sat down and started to polish his gold-framed glasses. Whenever he wished to think hard, he either did that or blew his nose.

'Who told you that?'

'It's all over the town, sir. Naturally, when the workmen don't know whether or not they're going to draw their wages at weekend, someone puts two and two together.'

'Very well. The company is, at present, financially embarrassed.'

'Dependent on the bank for its continued survival?'

'You seem to know a lot about it.'

'It's common knowledge in the town, sir.'

'Right then. What you say is true.'

'How much do they owe the bank?'

'That, too, will come out sooner or later. I'll tell you in confidence, then. Five thousands pounds.'

'Secured?'

'Yes and no. I dealt with the matter when security was deposited. Whether or not such security was full cover for the loan is doubtful. Is that all?'

'Could I ask why it is doubtful, sir?'

Mr. Boycott sighed and went through the pantomime of blowing his nose again whilst he sorted things out in his mind.

'I'll explain. First, the main security was joint and several guarantees for three thousand pounds, later increased to five thousand, signed by all five directors. You know the significance of the term joint and several. It means if they can all pay up, they share the liability equally. If any of them can't, the rest are liable for the whole debt between them.'

'Could they all meet it?'

'No. None of them could. The lot of them together couldn't, except that...'

Mr. Boycott sighed again as though the whole thing were a bore.

'The Hoops, Fallows and Piper had put all they had in the company to keep it going. If the bank had decided to send in the bailiffs, their personal assets, furniture and such, together wouldn't have raised a thousand pounds. Fred Hoop's furniture belongs to his wife, as does his house. The others mortgaged their houses to the hilt in the past to provide ready cash for the company. Dodd occupied a house owned by his wife and the furniture is also hers.'

'The bank weren't very bright when they granted the loan, were they?'

'I don't know about that. They'll get all their money back. Lucky for them.'

'How will they manage that? I thought...'

'Let me finish.'

'I'm sorry.'

'At first, the directors of the Excelsior arranged for an overdraft of a thousand pounds. They signed a guarantee and, as I've said, could, all together, probably have raised that amount if necessary. Then they asked for more. Another two thousand. It was either that, or bust. The bank asked for a further guarantee to cover and for security to back the guarantee. There wasn't any, except a policy for £5,000 on the life of John William Dodd, recently taken out and of little value unless Dodd died. That was charged to the bank and the company agreed to pay the premiums instead of Dodd. Subsequently Roper allowed them to borrow up to £5,000, or a little more. Dodd's death will bring in five thousand pounds and that, plus other odds and ends should pay off the bank overdraft.'

Mr. Boycott started to cackle.

'I'm sure you won't start suspecting the bank of throwing in the dynamite. Banks don't usually make good their bad debts by killing off their clients, do they?'

'No, sir. But what would have happened if the company failed before Dodd died?'

'The bank estimated that by selling up the machinery and other assets they could raise enough to obtain repayment of the loan. I doubt it. You see, the property is on lease to Excelsior and belongs to the daughters of the former owner of the company, Mr. Henry Jonas, who left it to them on his death. The rest was in rather out-of-date machinery which would have sold at scrap prices. No; I admit the bank would have had a hard task in raising enough to see them clear.'

Mr. Boycott put on his bowler hat to indicate that whatever Littlejohn was going to do next, he himself was off.

'I must get to court.'

As he left the room, Tattersall entered. He must have been waiting on the mat with his news.

'We've been going into the matter of the dynamite. About three months ago, the explosives shed at the Rosealba quarries, near Evingden, was broken into and several sticks were stolen...'

'It might have been teddy-boys from the neighbourhood. It surely wasn't professional safe-crackers. They'd use something more efficient than dynamite. Have you had teddy-boy trouble locally?'

'Plenty. The new town's full of them.'

'Any previous cases of dynamiting in the locality?'

'No.'

'So, we're as far away as ever.'

'Wait a minute. I'm wrong. Somebody tried to dynamite the safe of the new Home Counties Bank in Queen Elizabeth Street, the main thoroughfare of the new town. It didn't come off. We were sure it was the work of amateurs but never caught up with them. I'll get the file.'

Tattersall rushed off as though someone had dropped a stick of dynamite in his pocket. You could hear him calling for men and files in the next room.

The file was a very ordinary affair. It revealed that on Sunday August fourth that year, the day before bank holiday, the new branch of the Home Counties Bank in Queen Elizabeth Street had been entered by forcing the back door, and the large cash safe dynamited without any success.

The new premises had been erected to serve the new town, the original ones being situated in the old part, now inconvenient for the business and shopping quarters. The centre of gravity of Evingden had shifted with the reorganisation and the wave of new population.

The new bank had opened in June and its cash and books were kept in large safes pending the completion of a strongroom, work on which had been held up for the arrival of the main door.

The attack on the safe, which was in the cellar, had obviously been the work of amateurs, who had used dynamite. Professionals would have normally worked with gelignite, a better medium for precise work. The file stated that the thieves had, according to the experts' report, not tackled the lock of the safe at all, but tried to blast it open by fixing a charge to the back of it.

No tools left behind, no fingerprints, not a thing to work on, except the ignorance of the operators.

This had led to enquiries at likely places for obtaining explosives. It had turned out that a short time before, the explosives room of Rosealba quarries at Baron's Sterndale had been broken into and about four sticks of dynamite taken from an already opened box.

The Rosealba quarries stood about two miles from Evingden on the Brighton side, and a mile from the main road. They were small and old-fashioned and mainly concerned with freestone. The owners and operatives were elderly and adhered to the use of dynamite, instead of more modern mixtures when occasions arose for blasting.

The case had gone no further. The file ended – or rather petered out – with a pencil comment of some senior officer who had read it before committing it to the archives.

> *Amateur work? Probably local small fry who decided to have a go at a bank, stole the explosives, cased the bank and then after getting inside, didn't know what to do with the safe.*

There were a few photographs in the file. The wrecked cellar with the unopened safe triumphant in the ruins. Then a time schedule, revealing that the charge had gone off at five o'clock in the morning and roused the neighbourhood. The police had arrived almost right away but neither they nor anyone else they'd interviewed had seen the operators. The whole thing was, from the point of view of the criminal profession, a dismal flop.

Littlejohn closed the file and then filled and lit his pipe. He wondered how long the case was going to hang fire. In any event, he didn't like cases involving explosives. All murder was dirty business, but blowing up a victim was the limit. It often involved other innocent parties and was particularly difficult to investigate. He remembered his own involvement, when an Inspector, in the I.R.A. 'S' plan crimes, and in a particularly nasty affair where a man had blown up his father in a bath-chair…

Someone had obviously blown up Dodd and involved his two innocent co-directors at the same time. Fallows and Piper were honest-to-goodness workmen with little in their lives to call down murder on them. Or so he'd been given to understand…

The file said so. Perhaps they'd better check it themselves.

He sent Cromwell out to do the job and decided, himself, to go and have a talk with Mrs. Hoop at her mother's in Brantwood.

Tattersall offered to go with him, but Littlejohn put him off. He felt he'd rather do it his own way, and besides, the inquest on Dodd and his colleagues was due later in the day and Tattersall had the routine to prepare and the coroner to attend to.

'I'll manage, thanks. I'll take it easy. Who knows what might come out.'

'You'll find Bella at her mother's in Brantwood. Ever been to Brantwood? No? Four miles along the Brighton Road and then you'll see the signpost where you turn to the right and you'll find the village a mile along the side road. It's worth a visit. Quiet and still unspoiled, although the speculative builders and land sharks will soon ruin it if they get a chance. Old Morris Sandman, Bella's father, had bought a house in the main street there as a specula-tion, but died before he could sell it again. Mrs. Sandman moved into it and sold the flashy mansion he'd built for himself in Little Evingden. It's smaller and it's quieter in Brantwood, added to the fact that it was Mrs. Sandman's old home. She comes from a good local family.'

They offered Littlejohn a driver for the police car, but he pre-ferred to do it himself. He wished to take his time, to explore without being pushed by a companion or hampered by a schedule. He followed Tattersall's directions and took the busy Brighton road out of Evingden, turned at the signpost, and followed the by-road into Brantwood. A quiet, provincial little place which might have been a hundred miles from London. There was an old-fashioned pub in the high street and Littlejohn went inside for his lunch.

There was nobody else in the dining-room but a trio who looked like commercial travellers, men with their heads together telling tales or comparing notes on the possibilities of Brantwood. They looked up and stared hard at Littlejohn and then began their subdued conversation again.

On the opposite side of the street they were pulling down an old house and there was a sign in what had once been the garden. Blowers and Co. Demolitions.

Littlejohn was in no hurry. A waitress took his order, but the landlord felt he ought to greet him as well. A tall, fat suave man with a hoarse, fruity voice who looked like a promoted head-waiter.

'Would you care for a drink before the lunch, sir?'

'Yes, please. Sherry. The driest you've got. Care to join me?'

'That's very nice of you…'

He floated off for the drinks and was soon back wishing Littlejohn all the best.

'Does Mrs. Sandman live in Brantwood?'

'Yes. Just across the street in one of the old Georgian houses. You can't see it from here. A very nice place. I don't suppose it'll be here much longer. The main street's being developed and I guess before long she'll be made an offer she simply can't afford to refuse.'

'How long has she lived here?'

'Her husband died five or six years ago. Until then, they used it as a sort of country cottage, if you can call it such. They lived in Evingden, but Mr. Sandman, who used to be a good customer here, got possession of Pochins – that's the name of the house – through calling in a mortgage. He seemed to take a fancy to the place and he and his family came as often as they could, especially when they started to add the new town to Evingden. After his death, his widow sold the house at Evingden and came to live here.'

'Do you know his daughter, Bella?'

'Mrs. Hoop? Yes. She is living in Brantwood with her mother now. I hear there's been a bit of trouble in Evingden involving her husband's family. An explosion in which three men were killed. It's said she's come to her mother's until the affair blows over. But I don't know. She was over here most of her time before the explosion. There are rumours that she and her husband don't hit it off very well.'

He paused and looked hard at Littlejohn.

'You're from the police, aren't you? You're... don't tell me... Your picture was in last night's paper... Superintendent Littlejohn. Scotland Yard. Am I right?'

'Right first time.'

'Is Hoop suspected?'

'No. I'm on routine enquiries. I'm calling on Mrs. Hoop as a matter of form. Do you know her?'

'She comes here for lunch sometimes. Brings her mother now and then. Mrs. Hoop's getting a bit faded now, if you'll excuse the term, but when she was in her prime she must have been a smasher.'

'Has she any current admirers, would you say?'

The landlord smiled and thumbed his double chin.

'One of the chaps who got himself blown up at Evingden used to come to Brantwood pretty often to see her. His name was Dodd. A smooth piece of work, if you ask me. He stayed here overnight once or twice. That's how I knew his name. From the register. He often came in for a drink with her and now and then they'd take dinner together. He rather overdid it in telling people that there was nothing between him and Mrs. Hoop. He was financial direc-tor, he said, of a company in which Mrs. Hoop had interests and he came for instructions and to give her advice. He protested too much... Was it Bernard Shaw or Noël Coward who said that? At any rate, that's what he did. If he'd kept his mouth shut about it, nobody would have noticed it. As it was, all the town knew that he spent the night with her at Pochins every time her mother went to London for a day or two.'

They didn't get any further. A buxom, tired-looking woman entered the dining-room and told the landlord he was wanted on the 'phone. It was his wife who did most of the work whilst he talked. Now and then, when she felt he'd had long enough, she broke up the conversation by an imaginary telephone call.

Littlejohn finished his lunch undisturbed. Then he crossed the road to Pochins. It had all the appearances of a small town house and its history must have been interesting. Three steps flanked by railings overlapped the pavement and the developers who seemed to be taking possession of the locality must have been panting to remove them. The frontage was Georgian and there was a fine large door with a fanlight and a brass knocker. Littlejohn knocked.

There was a long delay. The curtains which completely screened the window to the left of the door moved, but Littlejohn could not see who was there, presumably eyeing him and deciding what to do about him. There was a bell-push on the door-frame; Littlejohn now used it. Somewhere far inside, he could hear the bell ringing. A door banged. Then the front door opened as far as an attached chain would allow it. He couldn't see who was behind it. Judging from the elderly voice, however, it might have been a maid or Mrs. Sandman.

'Yes, what is it?'

'Is Mrs. Fred Hoop at home?'

'She isn't available. You'll have to come again some other time.'

'Will you kindly let her know that Superintendent Littlejohn, of Scotland Yard, wishes to see her?'

There was a pause, as though whoever was behind the door was thinking out the next move. The chain was removed and the door opened. A tall, handsome, grey-haired elderly lady stood aside to let him enter.

'Mrs. Sandman?'

'Yes. My daughter has a caller and I'll have to ask if she can see you. Come inside.'

She was different from what he'd imagined she would be, the wife of a scrap merchant who'd made a fortune in government surpluses. She looked refined and spoke as though she'd had a good education. Her skin was pale and had a transparent look and her hands were long and fine.

They were standing in a long corridor painted white with black woodwork. There were some good pieces of furniture sparsely scattered about as though Sandman might have come across them in his search for surplus. It could have been a part of a private school or even a convent, and the elderly lady could have fitted in either.

'If you'll wait I'll see if she's free. I'm sorry to keep you. But my daughter has been going through a harrowing time over the past few days, as you are doubtless well aware.'

She left him standing in the hall and entered by the second door along the corridor. There wasn't a sound in the house, except the ticking of a large case clock midway along the passage. Nevertheless, he felt that someone was listening in the room nearby, someone who wondered who he was and why he'd called.

The noise of the town and the busy main street didn't penetrate the house, which gave him the impression that it hadn't changed much over the centuries since it was built. There was a strange atmosphere of dignity, almost mystery, about the place. He was sure that the demolishers busy not far away would put an end to that as soon as they could, and he felt sorry about it.

Mrs. Sandman was back. He hardly heard her approach. She moved quietly in keeping with the almost religious silence of the house.

'Could you tell me the reason for your call? My daughter's nerves are a little shaken. She feels...'

'I'm sorry to disturb you, madam, but I wish to ask her some routine questions about the affair at the Excelsior Joinery works. She is away from home and I've had to make a special journey to Brantwood. I'd be very much obliged if she could spare me a few minutes...'

Mrs. Sandman passed her fingers across her forehead.

'I wonder if you'd mind waiting a little while longer. I'll tell my daughter. No doubt we'll be able to arrange something.'

She seemed to be playing for time, as though in the room behind, the stage had to be set for his entrance. In the circumstances, however, he couldn't very well force the issue.

'I don't mind waiting...'

Mrs. Sandman vanished again, but first gave him a sad apologetic smile as though excusing herself for something she couldn't help or explain.

As he stood there trying to decide whether the framed cartoon over the small hall table was a genuine Rowlandson or a reproduction, he heard a vehicle draw up at the front door. He opened it quietly and found a large taxi at the kerb. A homely man in a peaked cap put his head out.

'Is he ready yet?'

'Who?'

'Mr. Hoop, of course. I was told to come back for 'im at one o'clock. It's past that time now.'

'Mr. Fred Hoop?'

'No. Mr. Tom.'

'I thought he was very ill.'

The man who had a pug-dog face was very good-humoured, but getting impatient.

'So did I, but he must have had a sudden turn for the better. I brought 'im here and now I'm due to take him 'ome. I've got some other runs to do when I get back to Evingden, so would you mind tellin' him I'm waiting?'

'I'll do that,' said Littlejohn and closed the door.

He was just in time. Mrs. Sandman appeared again. He thought it seemed too bad to have her hurrying backwards and forwards like a servant. Bella ought to have done it.

'My daughter will be free in a minute.'

He thanked her and looked gently at her.

'And if Mr. Thomas Hoop is with her, would you kindly ask him to remain until I've had a word with him, as well?'

She gave him a glance of reproach, as though he might have been prying into matters which didn't concern him during her absence, but she didn't answer.

'Please follow me…'

Quite a remarkable woman, Mrs. Sandman.

6

OLD TOM HOOP

T HE ROOM WAS QUITE OUT OF KEEPING WITH THE REST OF the place. The furniture and fittings were all modern and there was a monstrosity of a bar in one corner. Under the Adam mantel, a gas-fire had been installed and was burning full blast. There were hunting prints on the walls and Persian mats on the floor. The area was small and the paper on the walls further constricted the atmosphere. It had been the 'snug' of the late Mr. Morris Sandman.

Mrs. Sandman had been born in Pochins. It had belonged to her family for generations and Mr. Sandman had bought it from her cousin Anthony and given it to her as a birthday present. Actually, Sandman had foreclosed on a mortgage, but didn't tell his wife at the time. When he came to want to sell Pochins to a large retail store at a magnificent profit, his wife wouldn't agree and Sandman had died feeling frustrated to the end. His revenge had been to convert the nicest, cosiest room in the house into a bar in which he entertained his dubious friends.

Mrs. Sandman led the way and Littlejohn found an old man and a woman of uncertain age already in occupation. He assumed the man was Thomas Hoop and the woman Mrs. Fred. Mrs. Sandman introduced him. Neither of them offered to shake hands. He might have been the rate collector come for his dues or an agent collecting insurance premiums.

Mrs. Fred Hoop must have taken after her father. She didn't resemble her mother in the slightest detail. She was auburn, of medium height, voluptuously built, handsome and heavily made-up. She was expensively dressed and wore a lot of jewellery. If the stones in the rings on her fingers were genuine, she was well-off, however bankrupt her husband might be.

The old man in the chair by the fire didn't seem at home. His thin white hair was ruffled and his blue lips were pursed tightly. He was small and frail, clean-looking, with a flushed clear complexion and a grey moustache. He wore an expression of intense distaste.

As Littlejohn entered, he struggled to his feet.

'I'll be going. My taxi should be at the door and I've nothing more to say.'

'There's no hurry, dad. You'd better take a drink – as medicine, of course – before you go. It's cold outside.'

Tom Hoop gave his daughter-in-law a nasty look. The suggestion of paternity by the woman seemed objectionable and, added to that, he'd signed the teetotal pledge when a young man and had no intention of breaking it to please anybody, especially Bella Hoop.

'I hope you'll stay, sir. I have one or two matters to discuss with you and it might be convenient now.'

'I've nothing to say to the police.'

'We have something to say to you, sir. I hope you are feeling better.'

Littlejohn was surprised to find Tom Hoop in circulation at all. The last news he'd heard was that he was at death's door.

'I'm all right. What is it you've got to say? Say it and let me go. It's time I was home. I've been away long enough.'

He looked at the two women, standing uncertainly together between him and the fire.

'Anything I have to say will be in private.'

It was obvious that Bella, at least, wished to stay, but the compulsion in old Hoop's voice was too strong.

'Very well. Though I don't see why we shouldn't stay. After all we're concerned with all this.'

Bella Hoop had the husky voice of a contralto with laryngitis.

'Come along, Bella. We have plenty to do. Perhaps you two gentlemen will let us know when you're ready to go. We'll be in the kitchen.'

Mrs. Sandman said it very casually. A woman in full control of her feelings and quite unperturbed by the situation. She'd obviously learned after years with Sandman to take things as they came. They left the room, the mother leading the way and Bella following sulky and resentful.

'Well? What have you to say?'

Hoop slumped down in his chair, his arms hanging lightly, his head on one side supported by the wing. His eyes were pale blue and expressionless. His emotions were mainly expressed by flushes in his cheeks and by waving his arms about in ungainly jerks.

'Are you sure, sir, you are well enough to be out? You were, I believe, too ill when the disaster happened to take much notice of it.'

'I was not. I heard the explosion and was told all about it. I judged it unwise at the time to get out of bed and investigate.'

That was a cool one! Old Hoop was supposed to be on his last legs when the offices went sky-high!

'You were wise. I hear you had pneumonia, sir.'

'That's what they told me. It was a sharp attack of influenza and, I might add, you are in no position to tell me whether I was wise or not in staying in bed. To tell you the truth, I wish I hadn't. I'd probably have solved the problem of who did it if I'd been on the spot sooner.'

'Have you visited the place already?'

'Of course. I'm head of the company. It was my duty. I called there on my way here this morning. The fire brigade and police had reduced the place to such a shambles it was impossible to tell what had happened.'

To hide his smiles, Littlejohn took out his empty pipe and examined it fondly.

'Here, you can't smoke. My chest's bad enough without you puffing tobacco all over the place.'

'Sorry. Has the doctor agreed to your making this trip?'

'I didn't have a doctor. I don't believe in doctors and their wonder drugs which give you worse complaints than those they cure. I can very well look after myself. I'm quite a competent medical herbalist.'

Good! Old Hoop looked proud of it. Littlejohn felt he was dealing with a crank and decided to sheer away from health and illness. Otherwise they'd be all day at it and involved in herbs instead of explosives.

'Have you any idea why the murder was committed and who might have done it?'

'Your guess is as good as mine.'

'Suppose you tell me *your* guess, sir.'

'That's not my business.'

'Then I'll tell you a theory held by the local police. Forgive me if I'm blunt about it, but this is murder. It has been suggested that Dodd was having an affair with your son's wife… Please let me go on… That your son was too afraid of Dodd to challenge him to his face and deal appropriately with him. He therefore murdered him in Guy Fawkes fashion.'

Hoop hoisted himself to his feet in a sudden convulsive movement, trembling, flushed, stamping with rage.

'That's a damned impertinent lie! My son was nowhere near the office...'

He had to stop to fit in his false teeth, which he'd half-ejected by his shouting.

'That wouldn't be necessary in the case of explosives. The fire and explosion have destroyed and confused most of the contents of the building. Not the police and firemen, as you suggest. A time-device could have been used and our experts will probably find one when they've sifted the mass of rubbish. Please sit down. You're in no condition to get excited, sir.'

'I'll do as I like...'

All the same, he sat down panting.

'I'll do as I like and I advise you not to repeat that slander outside, or you'll regret it.'

'You must admit that Dodd and Mrs. Fred Hoop...'

'I admit nothing... I see now why you wanted Bella out of the way. To slander her behind her back.'

'*You* sent her packing, not I. I suggest you called here in an effort either to effect a reconciliation or enlist Mrs. Hoop's help in your son's defence.'

'You're wrong. He needs no defending. He was here when the explosion occurred. He'd been away from Evingden for over an hour.'

'That doesn't get over the theory of the time-device.'

'That theory is just a piece of balderdash to help you solve the case. You can't find a victim, so you're picking on an innocent man. I tell you, I'll move heaven and earth to beat and discredit you and your lies.'

'Your son called to ask his wife for further financial help for the company.'

'Mind your own business.'

'I've only to ask his wife to get the truth.'

'Oho! *She'll* tell you he was after her money. That would suit her. She tells everybody that. She's always harping on Fred being after her money. If she'd been a good wife to him, all this would never have happened and my son would have been able to concentrate on running the business successfully. As it is...'

It seemed obvious that old Hoop ran both Fred and the business. Littlejohn wondered, however, if he'd have allowed Fred to marry Bella if it hadn't been for her money. Perhaps that was it. Money. How Bella had come to marry Fred was quite a puzzle, too. The appeal of the ingenious, virile Dodd was quite understandable.

'Have you finished?'

'Not quite.'

'Then hurry up. I'm tired. I don't know why I'm staying here listening to your nonsense...'

'Perhaps, sir, it's because you're anxious to know exactly how far your son is incriminated.'

'Rubbish.'

The women must have been cooking in the adjacent kitchen. A smell of onions began to pervade the air. Then the door opened and Bella arrived, balancing a tray of drinks.

'Would you like some sherry, Superintendent?'

She handed Tom Hoop a glass of orange, which he refused.

'I don't want it.'

'Please yourself...'

Littlejohn almost said 'neither do I,' but it seemed too bad. He accepted a glass. It must have been Bella's choice; it tasted like the cooking variety. He felt it attack his stomach like strong acid.

'Thank you.'

She hesitated. 'Am I still *de trop*?'

'If by that you mean you aren't wanted, you're right.'

She stood in front of her father-in-law and a lock of hair fell across her face and made her appear more wild and ferocious. She looked ready to fling the orange drink in his face. She turned on her heel and went out without another word, banging the door behind her. Then she opened it again.

'You can tell your precious Fred not to call here again after money. There's none for him or any of you. Excelsior! That's a good one!'

Bang; and she was gone. An aroma of singed onions mingled with that of the exotic scent she left behind her.

'The baggage! The bitch!!'

Hoop drooled with temper and glared at the closed door for a while, as though she were still there.

'Anything else? I want to get out of this place. It's evil.'

'Had an official directors' meeting been called at the time the explosion occurred?'

'Are you still at it? You never stop. No. You can take it from me that Piper and Fallows were just unlucky. Whoever wanted to damage Dodd didn't know he'd arranged to meet Piper and Fallows at the office with the old old story of scratching round for money for the week's wages.'

'You are sure, then, that Dodd was the chosen victim?'

'Of course I am.'

'Why?'

'Why! Piper and Fallows were decent men without an enemy in the world. They were church deacons. All the workmen liked them and would have done anything for them. Their private lives were simple and blameless. It was that scoundrel Dodd they were after, believe me.'

'Who's *they*?'

'That's up to you. It certainly wasn't my son. He wouldn't...'

'He wouldn't have the guts. Is that what you're going to say, sir?'

It seemed a bit too bad, with the old man just holding himself together after his attack of flu or whatever it was. But he seemed intent on raising his son's stock uselessly. And Littlejohn had grown to know Fred Hoop. A nonentity you'd pass in the street without a second look, and forget. Intent on his wife's money, even to the extent of removing the good furniture in her house and hiding it somewhere in case the bank took it to meet his guarantee. A nobody who sheltered behind his lawyers and his dad. Perhaps with just enough courage and initiative to throw a stick of dynamite at his enemy, and then run.

'I've had enough. I've finished. You're insulting and offensive and I shall mention this to the local Chief Constable. You'll pay for this.'

He hoisted himself to his feet, picked up his ebony stick from the floor beside his chair, and beat on the table top with it. This brought in Bella like a jack-in-the-box. She must have been waiting behind the door.

'That's a good table! No need to take your bad temper out on the furniture...'

'Where's my hat and coat?'

'In the hall where you left them and you can put them on yourself...'

Her voice rose from that of the gravelly contralto to a shrill soprano. She was working up to a scene.

'When I married into your family, I told you you'd always be welcome in my home. I take that back. Never come here again. Neither you, nor your precious Fred, nor any of you. Specially tell your Fred to keep away. Him and his sticks of dynamite. Nobody's safe. It's like him to…'

She couldn't get the words out. She'd been winding herself up for hysterics and now they came. Yells and screams and then a hysterical heart attack. She clutched her abundant chest and said she was dying.

Mrs. Sandman entered serenely, slapped her hard on the face, and pushed her in an armchair.

'Control yourself, you silly!'

And Bella did.

Tom Hoop fought his way into his large overcoat with the help of Littlejohn.

'Leave me alone. I can manage to put it on myself. *Leave me alone!*'

Littlejohn almost asked Mrs. Sandman to hit old Tom on the jaw as well.

'Where's my hat?'

It had rolled under the hallstand and Littlejohn had to crawl on his hands and knees to rescue it. It was ridiculous. He bundled Tom Hoop quickly out to his taxi. As the driver was starting the engine, Fred Hoop arrived on his bicycle. Whatever else he was, Fred was a tryer! He'd come to raise the week's wages! The shop stewards at the Excelsior had told him what they'd do to him if he didn't.

Littlejohn left old and young Hoop in conference at the open door of the taxi. Whatever went on between them ended in Fred's defeat, for he didn't ring the bell at Pochins.

Littlejohn was indoors again, interviewing the two women this time.

Bella had recovered from her hysterics and was trying to behave as though she'd never had them. She offered Littlejohn more sherry, but he said he'd rather not, thank you, as he was really on duty.

'Your husband was here, I gather, at eight o'clock on November 8th, the time of the explosion in Green Lane.'

'Yes. He arrived about half-past seven. I really ought to refuse to give him an alibi, you know. He was so beastly to me.'

Littlejohn was nettled at the coy way in which she said it. Did she expect him to coax it out of her?

'You have no choice, Mrs. Hoop. If you don't care to answer me now, you could be called upon in court under oath if your husband were accused.'

She didn't seem interested in the legal niceties of the matter.

'The sacrifices I've made for him since we were married. It was bad enough taking on a ridiculous name like Hoop. But there was worse…'

Mrs. Sandman thought it time to intervene.

'Superintendent Littlejohn is merely asking you to confirm that Fred was here, Bella. If you don't wish to do so, then I will. He was certainly here, Mr. Littlejohn.'

'Thank you. He came to ask for help in providing wages for the men at Excelsior?'

Bella Hoop shrugged and her ear-rings flashed.

'Among other things. He tried to blackmail me into signing a cheque. He finally said he was in a position to divorce me. He said awful things, lies, about me and John. That was after he'd eaten his supper. He took care to do that before he became offensive. Otherwise I'd have sent him away hungry.'

'John is Mr. Dodd, Superintendent. And I don't think the Super-intendent is interested in...'

Bella was determined to tell Littlejohn the lot. She shouted her mother down.

'He said he was going to dismiss John Dodd and start divorce proceedings unless I gave up my friendship with him...'

Mrs. Sandman's lips tightened. It was evident that she herself thought the friendship was a broad one.

'I told him to get on with it. There are no children to think about, except John's, of course. I told my husband that without John, the whole Excelsior business would collapse.'

As if it hadn't collapsed already.

'I also said he was getting no more money from me. It would only go where all the rest I'd lent him had gone. Gone with the wind...'

She made a butterfly gesture in the air with her hand, presum-ably supposed to denote the flight of her capital.

She'd got herself confused. It could be assumed that Dodd had dissipated the money Fred had raised. That fact didn't seem to dawn on her.

'What time did your husband leave here?'

'Just after nine.'

'Without the money, I assume.'

'Of course. He even had the nerve to approach mother for a loan.'

Mrs. Sandman said nothing. She seemed mainly anxious to get it over and remove Bella from the stage.

'Had Mr. Dodd any enemies to your knowledge?'

'He certainly had Fred, who was an extremely jealous husband and couldn't even stand me to speak to another man. He would have kept me under lock and key almost if I'd allowed him...'

She lowered her voice as though about to impart an important secret.

'Have you ever read Proust, Superintendent?'

Neither had she! She had heard of him recently for the first time at a lecture at the Ladies' Luncheon Club. Her mother sighed. Bella was at it again and in full spate.

'No? There was a girl called Albertine. Proust actually locked her up in his house because he couldn't bear any other man to see her...'

Mrs. Sandman gave her a despairing look. Bella had been like this since she was a little girl. Playing a part all the time. When the idea of being a bride appealed to her, she'd taken Fred Hoop because the man of her choice hadn't come up to scratch. And when she'd got bored and the idea of a lover seemed fashionable, she'd flung herself in the arms of a second-rate nonentity like John Willie Dodd. Now, she was imagining herself as a prisoner of the jealousy of Fred Hoop!

'The Superintendent isn't interested in Proust at present, Bella. He is simply asking you if Dodd had any enemies. Fred wasn't likely to kill him out of jealousy for you...'

She actually laughed at the idea.

'Well, I was only trying to explain. John's wife doesn't understand him either, but I'm sure she doesn't hate him.'

'Had Dodd plenty of money?'

'He had invested his all in the company.'

'And yet, I'm told he managed to live very comfortably. Rather different from his co-directors and the workmen in the factory.'

Bella brushed it aside.

'We never discussed those things.'

'Did you ever lend money to Dodd?'

'Certainly not. How could you ask? He had his pride!'

Littlejohn could imagine it. Dodd asking for a fiver in the middle of a clandestine meeting!

'I think he had means… perhaps investments. He never seemed short of pocket-money. Mr. Roper at the bank was a great friend of his. Perhaps he helped him with investments. I remember once, when we were lunching together… We used to meet sometimes to discuss Excelsior affairs… I'm a large shareholder, you know. So is mother. It was useless trying to get any information from Fred. He was hopeless in financial matters…'

'But Dodd never met *me* and gave *me* lunch whilst he reported on his stewardship…'

Mrs. Sandman said it in a tired voice.

'Where was I? As I was saying, when we lunched once together, John pulled out a new five-pound note and said in his humorous way, "Good old Roper", as though the banker had given it to him.'

They all looked blankly at each other. Littlejohn didn't even know whether the little exhibitionist was telling the truth or a pack of lies. Judging from Mrs. Sandman's face it was the latter.

'I think that will be all, then. Thank you both for your patience. I'll call again if I may should anything further crop up.'

'Do that, Superintendent. We will always be glad to see you…'

Bella extended her hand limply to indicate the audience was at an end.

Mrs. Sandman saw him to the door.

'I'm sorry this has taken so much of your time, Superintendent. Bella is a little overwrought. Things of the past few days, you know…'

'I understand. Thank you again, Mrs. Sandman.'

As he made his way back to his car, he realised that Bella had expressed no regret, shown no grief about Dodd or any of the other innocent victims of this tragedy. Not a tear, not a sympathetic reference. She took it all as a part of the game.

There were other sensations that day.

Fred Hoop struck oil when the bank agreed to find the elusive wages for the Excelsior workmen, but when he arrived home from Brantwood, old Tom Hoop had a heart attack and died.

OVERDRAFTS

T HE BRANCH OF THE HOME COUNTIES BANK IN THE OLDER
part of Evingden had been built in 1898 and still bore on its
cornice, chiselled in the stone, the coat of arms of the East Sussex
Bank, which the Home Counties had absorbed in 1920. It was a
cramped and inconvenient building for modern purposes, one day
to be superseded by the fine new office in the new part of the town,
already opened, flourishing, and full of every modern convenience.

That was the trouble with George Frederick Handel Roper, the
manager of the 1898 branch. They hadn't made him chief of the
new branch when they opened it. At first, he'd expected the directors would appoint him manager of both offices. Instead, they'd
left him in the lurch in his stuffy little room in the old decaying
part of the town. He'd only four years to go before he retired. He
resented the snub.

Littlejohn found Mr. Roper sitting in his office contemplating
statistics which showed that his business was declining. People
were gradually moving away from the old to the more pleasant
and commodious branch in the high street and Caffrey, the new
manager, was doing his best to keep up the one-way traffic. Already,
Caffrey had a staff of seven; Mr. Roper's personnel now stood at six,
including himself, and Head Office were talking of taking another
man away from him.

Mr. Roper received Littlejohn cordially, for he thought he was a
new client bringing a new account. When he learned he was from

the police, he lapsed into his habitual disappointed lethargy and rather brusquely offered him a seat.

The room was dark and shabby and the carpet was a bit thread-bare. The windows were set high in the walls and from where they were sitting they could merely see the roofs of old buildings and the square tower of the church of St. Michael and All Angels. It was dismal and depressing at that time of year. The branch was running down like the management and soon the residue of the business and everything else would be transferred to the new premises.

'I've not much time to spare. We're very busy at present. Staff shortages play the very devil...'

He was a portly little man who'd been at the same office in Evingden as cashier, then manager, for twenty-five years. He had started his management with great expectations. A major in the army with a decoration in the second war, he'd been full of initiative and a sense of his own importance. But somehow the great expec-tations hadn't blossomed. The same office, the same walk to and from home daily, the same customers, the same accounts through all the years had gradually run down his spirits and his temper.

Now, he was marking off the days to his retirement with grim and bitter regularity on his private calendar and hoping that noth-ing would happen to trip him up before the race was ended. He didn't even seem curious or excited by the visit from the police.

Mr. Roper wore a dark green worsted suit of a slightly racy cut. On a hook in the corner hung his bowler-hat. It was of an obsolete sporting style and had a ventilator like a sieve on top. It was a memento of his palmy days when he'd moved proudly with his first wife among the county people who banked at his office. They had since left Evingden for quieter country. He hadn't been as successful socially since his first wife died. The second was more aggressive and ambitious and had quarrelled with many of his old friends. His business had suffered through it and he drank more heavily to forget things. When he faced realities, Mr. Roper had to admit that he'd missed promotion through indifference; sometimes he even admitted incompetence as well.

He brushed his moustache thirstily. He had a dim impulse to offer Littlejohn a drink and then he decided against it. He'd better be official instead of sociable. He put on his military manner.

'Well? What is it?'

'Excelsior Joinery, sir.'

Mr. Roper frowned. It was a name which had lost him some sleep over recent years. Now... Well, it was all over now. He'd get his money back, but only by a sheer stroke of luck.

'What of them?'

'I called to ask if you could help us about the financial situation of the company, sir.'

'I can't divulge any information whatever on that score. It's private and confidential. The bank never does that. Not even to the police. As a senior officer, you ought to know it.'

'We know quite a lot already.'

'How much?'

Mr. Roper suddenly softened. He produced whisky, soda and glasses from a cupboard in his desk.

'Will you join me in a drink, Superintendent? We might discuss this informally.'

'No, thank you, sir. I'm on duty.'

'Of course. Mind if I have one? This business has shaken me.'

He filled his glass and drank heavily.

'Ah... Four directors out of five dead...'

He snapped his fingers.

'Dead. Just like that. We never know, do we? I've just heard old Hoop's gone. That leaves Fred Hoop all alone with the lot. Have you found out anything fresh about the explosion, Superintendent?'

'Only that we think it was murder. As far as we can discover, the company wasn't in the habit of keeping explosives in its office. It looks as if the dynamite was planted there or thrown in. It's local knowledge that the Excelsior was heavily indebted to your bank. And also that the bank will lose nothing, as the loan was secured.'

Mr. Roper drank again, wiped his moustache on a silk hand-kerchief and looked grave.

'It was a jolly good job I insisted on being fully covered. Recent events will probably see the end of the company. It's been in its death-throes for some time. This will finish it.'

Mr. Roper looked to be in the throes of something, too. He had turned ashen as though contemplating the situation if he hadn't been fully secured.

'It makes me ill to think of it. I may be on the way to recover-ing all the loan, but I never wanted it this way. I'd rather have lost the lot. It was damned bad luck on them all. I feel sorry for Fred Hoop. He's not of the calibre to see things through. It'll kill him if he's not careful.'

'What was your opinion of Dodd?'

Mr. Roper looked hard at Littlejohn.

'It's difficult talking of one who's not yet... not even in his grave, isn't it?'

He poured himself another drink and took a good swig of it.

'I mean... Well...'

'I understand. But this is very necessary, sir. We want to find out who killed Dodd and his friends. The sooner the better. Every day counts in a case like this.'

'If you ask me, you ought to be looking among the roughs in the overspill population. We've imported a lot of toughs of late. In my view they'd been trying to blast the safe at the Excelsior office, had been disturbed by the directors' arrival, and had to leave the explosives, which went off. That's my opinion for what it's worth.'

'We aren't neglecting that angle, sir. We were speaking of Dodd.'

Mr. Roper swallowed hard. At first, Littlejohn thought he was going to protest again.

'I didn't care for Dodd, I must confess. But I never wished him an end like this. He was really the ruin of Excelsior. Took too many risks, spent too much money...'

'Did he bank with you, sir?'

'Yes.'

'You lent him money personally?'

'Against security, yes. Now and then. He was extravagant, but I never let him take more than he could secure. I shouldn't be telling you this, you know, but I want to see justice done, and if I can help...'

'We know the directors guaranteed a loan of several thousands by your bank and that all of them, except Dodd, had little in the way of resources to meet their commitment. In fact, the bank will have to depend on Dodd's life policy to recover their money.'

Mr. Roper was on his feet.

'Look, Superintendent. The situation was confidential and sacred. Yes, sacred to the bank. I hope the police haven't been questioning my staff behind my back.'

'No, sir. I'll tell you candidly where the information came from. It was from Mr. Boycott, the company's lawyer.'

'I see. A bit indiscreet of him, I must say. He talks too much. Professional secrecy isn't lightly to be broken. All the same, your information is correct.'

'Had Dodd not died, the life policy would have been worth very little to the bank and they would have suffered in consequence.'

Mr. Roper changed colour to grey again and drank more whisky.

The very thought of it! They were in a real mess!

'There were, of course, the machinery and debts, which would have yielded quite a considerable sum of money.'

'Were they charged to the bank?'

'No. But in a liquidation…'

Mr. Roper seemed uncertain about his facts and paused. Littlejohn was in no way qualified to carry on a financial argument with him. He wished his friend, Horace Flight, of the Fraud Squad, had been there.

There seemed little else to be said. It had reached the stage where as far as the case was concerned, Littlejohn and Roper were sitting eyeing each other across the table and saying nothing. Mr. Roper was looking unsteadily, too, as though he wished Littlejohn would take himself off.

'Anything more?'

'I don't think so, sir.'

'Then I'll get on with my work. It's nearly time to close and I've a lot of letters to dictate yet.'

His desk was empty, but perhaps Mr. Roper carried it all in his head.

In any case, Littlejohn wished to call at the other branch of the Home Counties Bank, the new one in the new town. So, he thanked Mr. Roper, bade him good-day and hurried away.

He was just in time. The junior of the new office was closing the door.

'Is the manager free?'

The junior was a bright boy and recognised Littlejohn from his picture in the *Evingden Examiner*. He was going steady with a girl who collected autographs and almost asked Littlejohn to oblige. Then he decided perhaps he'd better not. A famous detective's signature among those of a lot of pop singers didn't seem appropriate...

'Yes, *sir*.'

He even forgot to close the door in his haste to announce the visitor and two belated customers sneaked in, much to the annoyance of the chief cashier, who pointedly left his till and closed the bank himself.

It was an up-to-date branch. The front was almost entirely of glass and the public, honest and bandit alike, could see all that went on. Sometimes, the impoverished of the town would pause there for quite a while, looking in at the piles of cash, like children, hungry and standing over the savoury grid outside an eating-house. The interior walls were painted and papered in a variety of startling colours and the manager's room had wallpaper of pink, blue and yellow with a peach-coloured carpet and scarlet upholstery. Mr. Caffrey, the manager, leapt up from the midst of it all and warmly shook Littlejohn's hand.

'Good afternoon, Superintendent Littlejohn. Very pleased indeed to meet you.'

Littlejohn might have been a potential big customer.

Caffrey was only thirty-eight, which was a thorn in Mr. Roper's flesh. Tall, slim, swarthy and highly polished, he had been taught banking and all that went with it from A to Z at his bank's staff college. He was a man with a future and some said he would one day be General Manager of the whole set-up. He indicated bottles of sherry in a cupboard on the wall.

'Sweet or dry?'

Without more ado he filled up.

'Good health and success to your case, sir. It's the queerest affair that's ever happened in Evingden.'

He knew all the history of the town, too. Useful as a talking-point in meeting established citizens.

'I've just been to see Mr. Roper about Excelsior Joinery. They're his clients...'

'Yes, indeed. Poor old Roper. I believe they've led him a bit of a dance. They've been in a poor way for some time. Between you and me, sir, their cheques have been bouncing all over the town. I wondered if someone was trying a bit of fire-raising and did it too thoroughly. There seems no other explanation for the tragedy at their works.'

'At any rate, it has solved Mr. Roper's problems. I hear the bank would have suffered a bad debt otherwise.'

'Yes. I know. I heard all about it from Handel. That's Roper's first name. His father was a prominent local musician and called his son after his favourite composer. The whole works... George Frederick Handel Roper...'

'He's a local man, then?'

'Yes. Born and bred in Evingden. Strictly *entre nous*, he's like the old premises he occupies. A bit *passé*.'

'Are you a native, too?'

'Yes. I started under Handel Roper in the old office. I've been around a bit since those days. He was quite a promising man then. He never got over his first wife's death. Married again to a bit of a tartar. He'd only one daughter, the apple of his eye. When he brought home his new wife, Benita, the daughter, packed up and left. She married a chimney-sweep in the Isle of Wight. Not the black-faced type; the sort who uses a vacuum-cleaner up the chimney and runs a profitable company.'

Mr. Caffrey laughed heartily and then grew solemn.

'Poor Handel has had a packet of late.'

'Does he stand high in the bank's regard?'

'Old-fashioned. He's spent most of his career in Evingden. A mistake, you know. Makes it that you can't say No to old friends and associates. It leads to bad debts, if you aren't very careful.'

'Perhaps the Excelsior loan was an example.'

'I'll tell you in confidence…'

Mr. Caffrey looked disposed to tell Littlejohn quite a lot. He was intoxicated by the idea of collaborating with Scotland Yard.

'In confidence, he's been on the mat a time or two at Head Office for risky lending and bad debts. I've been asked myself by H.O. how he stands locally. It amounts to this. If he misbehaves much more and loses any more money for the bank, he might be demoted and lose his managerial position. It would be a tragedy for Roper. He's due to retire in a year or two and that might greatly affect his pension. Head Office are only keeping the old branch in Evingden open out of regard for Handel Roper. When he goes, all the business will be transferred here.'

'So, a bad debt with Excelsior might be very damaging.'

'It would indeed. Especially as H.O. were angry about his making the loan in the first place. He granted the overdraft first, I gather, and told H.O. afterwards.'

Mr. Caffrey paused and shook his head almost reproachfully, as though inwardly chiding himself for talking too much.

'I hope you'll keep this information to yourself, sir. I'm only giving it in the hope that it will help your investigation. It might assist you in judging the nature of the Excelsior business and the mess they are in.'

'They're in a bigger mess, now. They've only one director left. Fred Hoop. Is he a customer here?'

'Yes. That's all I can say. I'm not allowed to disclose his financial position. You understand?'

'Of course.'

Mr. Caffrey might just as well have said Fred Hoop was on his uppers. Probably another issuer of bouncing cheques.

'I believe you, too, had an explosion here not long ago.'

'I'll say we had. A silly business. The local police haven't been able to get to the bottom of it yet. It struck me as either a crazy prank, or else the work of an apprentice burglar testing his skill with dynamite. He didn't even crack the safe. But he was cute enough to leave no trace behind him.'

'There may be some connection between your explosion and that at Excelsior.'

'A sort of rehearsal?'

Mr. Caffrey laughed heartily again.

'Maybe. Or something more crafty: the murderer just spreading false clues for the police.'

'Indeed! I'd not thought of that.'

Outside in the office, strange machines sounded to be squaring off the accounts for the day and balancing and putting away the cash.

'Your affair occurred over the weekend, didn't it?'

'Yes. Sunday morning when there was nobody about. The usual weekend snatch... or attempted snatch. That is, if it was genuine.'

Mr. Caffrey looked troubled.

'Where could anybody buy the dynamite in a place like this...? Perhaps they could steal it from a quarry, let's say. There's only one in this locality. It's a few miles in the Brighton direction from here. The Rosealba quarry. Sandstone, you know. They blast now and then. They bank here. Transferred to me from the City and Counties Bank when we opened in Evingden.'

'Who owns it?'

'A family affair. People of the name of Pochin.'

'Pochin? I've heard that name before. Yes. A house. In Brantwood.'

'You've hit it, sir. The Pochins came from there. The house is occupied at present by Fred Hoop's mother-in-law. She was a Miss Pochin before she married a fellow named Sandman. Morris Sandman. He made a fortune selling government surplus. Bit of a dark horse. Everybody was surprised when Miss Pochin married him, I believe. But, in love, there's no accounting for taste, is there? It's said Sandman ended up financially interested in the Rosealba quarries. Put them on their feet, in fact. That was before he married Miss Pochin.'

A real mine of information! Littlejohn wondered where Caffrey got it all from.

'Is Mrs. Sandman still interested in the family concern?'

'Yes. She's a director.'

There was a tap on the door. The bright new junior entered apologetically. He gave Littlejohn an admiring smile and then addressed himself to his boss.

'Sorry, sir. Sorry to interrupt. Mr. Alderman Vintner wishes to see you. It's urgent.'

The alderman didn't wait. He blundered in after the junior. A huge, heavy-jowled man, with a red face, angry little eyes under shaggy brows, snub nose, thick, hanging underlip. He seemed to have difficulty in moving his huge bulk and punted himself along with a heavy ebony stick. He was evidently bent on bullying Caffrey, but drew himself to a standstill, like a huge vessel entering dock, when he saw Littlejohn.

'Hullo. It's you, is it? I thought you'd gone. Littlejohn, isn't it?' He had a deep, suffocated bronchial voice.

'Yes, sir.'

Mr. Caffrey hurried to introduce them.

'Never mind introductions, Caffrey. My name's Vintner. Alderman Vintner. I'm also a J.P. And I'm on the Watch Committee. I know you, Superintendent, because I've had you pointed out to me. I saw you come into the bank, but I thought you'd have gone by this.'

He gave Caffrey a questioning look as though expecting him to divulge what it was all about.

Littlejohn took him up.

'I called for a chat about the explosion here some time ago. I've finished now and won't take up any more of Mr. Caffrey's time.'

He shook hands with Caffrey and thanked him. The alderman waited impatiently. He didn't seem to like the good terms on which the banker and Littlejohn appeared to be. He suddenly thrust his face close to Littlejohn's.

'I don't know why Scotland Yard need to interfere in this matter. We've a perfectly good police force of our own here. First class, I call it, and, as a J.P., I'm in a position to know. To my mind, it's ridiculous calling you in.'

'Good afternoon, gentlemen.'

Littlejohn didn't even bother to argue. As he left, Alderman Vintner was lowering his huge bulk in one of the customers' chairs.

He'd probably have taken the manager's seat if Caffrey hadn't been too quick for him. He looked that sort.

Half an hour later, as he was drinking tea with Tattersall, Littlejohn was disturbed by the telephone. It was Caffrey again.

'I'm just calling to apologise for the discourteous way in which I let you go from the bank, sir. Alderman Vintner is a bit of a tartar and, although he isn't a customer here – he banks at our other branch – he thinks he owns the whole bank. I'm sorry he pushed you out so rudely.'

'Don't worry, Mr. Caffrey. I was ready for off. Forget it. And thank you for all the help you gave me.'

'You might be interested to know why Alderman Vintner called. He wished to know why *you'd* called.'

'What did you tell him?'

'Just what you told him. About the explosion. Nothing more. He said he'd a right to know things, as when the murderer was caught, he'd come before him on the bench.'

'Who *is* this Vintner?' Littlejohn asked when it was all over. He told Tattersall what it was about.

'I like his dam' cheek. A self-opinionated boaster, indiscreet and foolish in a crowd and a particular swank in the presence of women. He still thinks he owns the town. A big frog in a little pool before the extension. Now that the town has grown so much, nobody but himself thinks he's anybody.'

'Why is he so interested in me, though? His excuse was a bit thin.'

'I guess he thinks that as one of Dodd's family, in a matter of speaking, he's a right to know what goes on. He has a big plumber's and ironmonger's shop in the old town. He's rolling in money, I believe. The new town's been a godsend to him. New houses need ironmongery and plumbing, don't they? Like hell, they do.'

'A plumber. Mrs. Dodd was a plumber's daughter...'

It sounded like a nursery rhyme!

'That's it. Vintner is her father.'

'But when I met him at the bank, he made no mention of it. He didn't behave as though there were a death in the family, either.'

'He wouldn't. He hated Dodd. I don't need to tell you that Dodd was a philanderer. His marriage with Betty Vintner was a shotgun affair. After the marriage, Dodd was soon back at his old games with the women. It galled Vintner. He forbade Dodd ever to enter his house again, after the way he'd treated his daughter. He never mentions Dodd. In fact, far from mourning Dodd's decease, I'll bet the alderman's glad.'

'I heard Mrs. Dodd's father had two sons, although I didn't know it was Vintner.'

'Yes. They left Evingden years ago. Started a building company in the West End of London.'

'What about putting the alderman and his sons on our list of suspects?'

Tattersall laughed brokenly.

'Him! You mean he might have killed Dodd for what he did to Betty? No. He's quarrelled with Betty, too, and cut her off with a shilling. Not only did she persist in sticking to Dodd in spite of her father's advice to divorce and be rid of him, but her mother, when she died, mortally affronted old Vintner by leaving all she had – it wasn't much – to Betty, instead of to Vintner himself. Betty invested it in the Excelsior, I believe. That was enough for the alderman. There was a hell of a row and that was that. He'd no reason for killing Dodd. You can cross him off. After his quarrel with Betty, he'd give no support to his daughter, however badly Dodd treated her.'

Instead, Littlejohn put the alderman on the list.

8

POLYDORE

JOHN ROBERT PIPER AND HIS WIFE HAD LIVED IN THEIR OWN house, mortgaged to the bank, of course, in Railway Terrace, Evingden. It was a small, semi-detached place with a garden which Piper had made his hobby before the affairs of the Excelsior had driven it from his mind. All that was left of the garden was the wreckage of summer, dead and gone blooms, rotting Michaelmas daisies, overgrown paths and a solitary rosebud dying on a leafless stem. The property fronted on the railway line and Piper had once boasted he never needed a clock to tell the time as the trains did it for him.

When Cromwell arrived, he found Mrs. Piper and her daughter there.

'You're lucky to find us at home. Mother's just come for her black clothes. It's the funeral the day after tomorrow. She's taken all this badly. It's hard enough dying in one's bed, but to die like my dad did...'

Mrs. Flowerdew, *née* Piper, then burst into tears and between the sobs managed to invite Cromwell indoors.

'She's living at our house at present. To stay on in this empty place after what she'd been through would be unbearable...'

She didn't even ask the purpose of Cromwell's visit. His dark austerely cut clothes and white linen often caused him to be mistaken for a nonconformist parson. Mrs. Flowerdew thought he'd called to tender condolences and comfort. She offered him a chair whilst she went to find her mother, who could be heard forlornly rummaging about in the room overhead.

Cromwell looked around him. A comfortable living-room with traces of the dead man still scattered about. A cold pipe in an ash-tray, carpet slippers near the hearth, books, magazines... Family photographs and out-of-date pictures on the walls, and a large castor-oil plant flourishing in front of the window.

There was silence upstairs, as though mother and daughter were indulging in a whispered conference. Then they began to descend, one very slowly, and the other helping her.

Mrs. Piper was a thin, white-haired woman, pale and stricken-looking. She seemed surprised when, instead of the local Methodist minister, she encountered Cromwell. She and her daughter looked afraid and resentful after Cromwell introduced himself.

'This is hardly the time, is it? I thought the inquest was over.'

'It was deferred, Mrs. Piper. It will be re-opened when the police report is ready.'

'But they won't keep bothering me, will they? It brings it all back and I can't stand much more of it.'

'That's really why I'm here. To save you trouble. Do you feel able to answer a few questions to help us? Please accept my condolences.'

Mrs. Piper wept a little. Her daughter comforted her as best she could, casting glances full of reproach at Cromwell. Mrs. Flowerdew must have been the child of her parents' middle age. Her mother looked well past sixty; her daughter in her late twenties. She wore navy-blue jeans and a light blue jumper which didn't go well with her ample figure.

'I'm sure I'll do what I can, because it's not knowing how it happened that is so upsetting. If I only knew how and why they did it to my husband. Why would anybody want to do it? The police said it couldn't have been an accident.'

'We're trying to find the answer. Meanwhile, had your husband any enemies… anybody who would wish him ill?'

Mrs. Piper was overcome and shed more tears at the thought of her husband's kindly nature and that anybody might wish him harm. Her grief turned to fury at the thought of it and she looked ready to denounce Cromwell for suggesting it.

'He hadn't an enemy in the world. That's why I still say it must have been an accident. I told my husband when all this started at the Excelsior that Dodd would never do him any good. But my husband was that way. Always looked for the best in people. Even Dodd. And look where it's landed him. And me. Every penny we had was locked up in that bankrupt company. My husband always used to say it would turn out all right. This house will, like as not, have to be sold to pay off the bank for the bond my husband signed. I won't have a roof over my head and I'll be dependent on a few pounds a week widow's pension. It's not fair…'

Mrs. Flowerdew thought it time to put in her motto before her mother broke down again.

'You'll live with us, mother, and while I'm alive, you won't want anything.'

'It's not the same.'

Mrs. Piper didn't seem grateful.

'Did your husband leave a will, may I ask, Mrs. Piper?'

She bridled.

'I don't see that's any business of yours. If he did, it's worth nothing. He'd nothing to leave.'

'Has the will been found?'

'Whatever you do in the police, it's not decent worrying ordinary people by investigating a man's money and how he left it until he's been properly laid to rest. The funeral's the day after tomorrow and I'll thank you...'

'I'm sorry, Mrs. Piper, but I just wondered where the will was. It's rather important to us, you see. It may help us in finding the cause of his death. That's the only reason I asked.'

He said it in so contrite a way that Mrs. Piper relented. Afterwards, she told her fellow mourners at the funeral what a nice young man Cromwell was.

'He kept it with his private papers in his desk. I'll have to open it to get at the deeds of the grave. I might as well do it now.'

She took a bunch of keys from a drawer in the sideboard and with one of them unlocked the top of an oak bureau in one corner. She emerged with a cheap tin box with the label of a well-known brand of biscuits still upon it, and placed it on the table. Then she opened it and began to turn out the contents. She apologised for the box.

'He'd never much in the way of valuables and never took much care of what he had got. I used to tell him burglars wouldn't have much trouble if they got in here...'

Her voice trailed away as she took out various items from the box. The will was there with a lot of other papers. It was completely in favour of his wife and on a home-made form. There didn't seem to be much else of value, as far as Cromwell could see. A gold watch and chain, a locket, a ring or two, a bank passbook, probably with little or no balance.

Mrs. Piper talked to herself. She seemed to be brooding on past history as one thing after another of the contents of the box came to the light of day and jogged her memory. She flung aside a number of old papers.

'He'd accumulated a lot of rubbish in the box that he didn't seem to wish to get rid of for sentiment's sake. There's an empty envelope my husband must have kept because it's got his father's handwriting on it. The deeds of his father's house were in it. The house was in the country in those days. Now it's been pulled down and a chain store put up in the main street of the new town, where the house used to stand. My husband inherited it from his father and sold it for £800 and put the money in the Excelsior. Not long after that the new town developed and land went up in price like mad. I remember Bob, that's my husband, saying it would have brought in five or six times what he sold it for if he'd only known about the new town scheme.'

'Who did he sell it to?'

'A friend of John Willie Dodd's. Dodd kept pressing Bob to invest in the Excelsior. He said it was a gold mine. He was a good talker and persuaded my husband, who was no businessman at all. So Bob sold his father's cottage. It had been let and Dodd had said he could get double or treble what he got in rent by investing the money in the Excelsior. I put £300 of my own in the firm, too. It's all gone. Every cent of it.'

'This friend of Dodd's. Who was he?'

'I don't remember, if I ever knew. Bob did all the business. Dodd said he knew someone who wanted a house in that neighbourhood, so one night my husband went off and sold it. A few weeks later he came home with proceeds in cash. Eight hundred pounds in one-pound notes.'

'Cash!'

'Yes. It seemed funny. We were both a bit surprised. My husband also was surprised that instead of a private person, the house had been sold to a company. My husband had asked Dodd about that and he said that his friend was employed by the company and that he was starting to work for them in Evingden and the company was buying the house for him to live in. It seemed reasonable.'

'Did you ever know the name of the company?'

'No. I was more interested in them paying in cash. It seemed funny. But there it was, in good pound notes and every cent of it went in the Excelsior.'

Cromwell made notes in his black book and Mrs. Piper and her daughter were much impressed.

'Can you tell me what your husband was doing at the Excelsior office on the night of the accident, Mrs. Piper?'

'I don't know. I only wish I did. I expect it was Dodd again, wanting more money for wages. Things had been going from bad to worse and Dodd had asked my husband a time or two if he couldn't raise any more money to save the company. Dodd made promises to repay all the extra he'd borrowed, temporarily, he said, when some bills had been paid by those who owed money to Excelsior. We never got it back. He was for ever pestering Bob. The night of the accident, he came to my husband as the works closed for the day and asked him to meet him at the office at seven-thirty. I don't know what it could have been about. Another of those silly directors' meetings where Dodd and old Tom Hoop did all the talking and ordering about and my husband and Dick Fallows simply agreed to what the others said and made themselves responsible for it. It was a scandal the way things were run.'

'You knew Dodd well?'

'Yes I did and I never liked him. It was a funny thing, but my husband seemed to trust him. I used to tell him he was no judge of character, trusting and believing all that a fellow like Dodd said and did. A man of no honour and shocking morals… I could tell you a thing or two. But we mustn't speak ill of the dead. My husband used to laugh at me when I complained about Dodd. He used to say he knew his way about the joinery trade and that what he did outside was his own business. My husband thought everybody was as honest as he was himself…'

'Well, Mrs. Piper, I'll not detain you any further. Thanks for your help. I'm very sorry about it all…'

He left the bewildered woman, with the open box still in front of her, poring over papers, stirring up old memories.

It wasn't far to the home of Richard Fallows, another director and victim of Excelsior; his house was two streets away from that of the Pipers, similar in construction, semi-detached with a long slope to the front door and a neglected garden in the front.

According to Cromwell's notes, Fallows was an old man, who had lost his wife a couple of years before and lived with an elderly housekeeper. He wondered if he'd find anybody at home. He needn't have worried.

When Cromwell beat on the knocker, there seemed to be a scrimmage as to who should answer the door. About three people at once sounded to be struggling to admit him. Then, the door burst open revealing what looked like the meeting of some private religious sect going on. The room inside was full of people in black clothes, men and women and children, all with their eyes fixed on the doorway.

Cromwell's black book said that the old housekeeper was called Henniker.

'Is Mrs. Henniker in?'

The man between Cromwell and the rest of the black throng wasn't going to be put off by that. He looked like a boxer in his

Sunday clothes. He even had a cauliflower ear. He seemed to have elected himself doorkeeper by sheer muscular strength.

'What's she wanted for? I'm the late Mr. Fallows's nephew. I'm in charge.'

He couldn't have used a worse opening gambit with Cromwell.

'Are you? Well, I'm here to see Mrs. Henniker. Is she in?'

Most of the throng behind the pugilist seemed delighted. He'd been throwing his weight about and though the rest resented it, none seemed prepared to challenge him.

'Yes. But…'

The boxer raised a huge hand.

'I want to see Mrs. Henniker. I'm from the police. Will you please stop arguing and ask her to show herself?'

There was a commotion as the police were mentioned. They invited Cromwell inside unanimously, the pugilist backed indoors defeated and was absorbed by the crowd, and an old woman in black with an apron over her skirt was thrust forward.

'Who wants me? As if I hadn't enough troubles without more people worryin' me…'

For all her lamentations, she was a white-haired motherly sort of woman. Cromwell felt like addressing her as 'Ma', but thought better of it.

'Might I have a word with you in private, Mrs. Henniker? I'm from the police.'

She gave him a scared look as though instinctively imagining he'd come to arrest her, and then closed the door of the vestibule, cutting him off from the crowd indoors, silent, listening to catch a word or two of what was going on. As soon as the door closed, shutting Cromwell and Mrs. Henniker in a receptacle little larger than a sentry-box, a hubbub immediately started in the rooms behind as the assembly exchanged views about why Cromwell was there at all and the ethics of the situation. To the intruder, it all sounded like a queer *danse macabre*.

'There's nowhere private in this house now. We'll have to talk here if you insist.'

'Who are that lot?'

She explained rather breathlessly that whereas Fallows and his wife had been childless, the good Lord had seen fit to more than compensate his two brothers, who had seven children and fifteen grandchildren between them. These two great families were rival factions for what they were sure was a wealthy birthright from their uncle. Scenting a will and money for distribution, they were now eagerly seeking their dues. The present gathering had arisen because each member of each family jointly and severally mistrusted the others to enter their uncle's house alone. 'It's easy to pick up odds and ends if you're not watched,' one had said.

There was only one of Fallows's brothers still alive and he had stolen and smoked one of his brother's cigars, for lack of anything else to filch. Unaccustomed to such strong luxury, he had collapsed half-way through it and had been carried upstairs and cast upon a spare bed to recover.

Having thus forcibly eased her feelings by the rigmarole, Mrs. Henniker asked Cromwell what he wanted to know.

'Did Mr. Fallows leave a will?'

She grimly jerked her head in the direction of the human cockroaches behind the closed door, which she had now locked to maintain privacy.

'If you know where it is, you'd better tell them and put them out of their misery. They've turned the place upside down and can't find one. I told them he often said he'd better make one, but never brought his mind to it. Which means that after all I've done for him since his wife died, I'll not even get a pound or two to remember him by. I don't know what I'm going to do. I'm nearly seventy and work at my age is hard to find.'

Cromwell was very sorry for her and he told her so, but he had a feeling that at any time the door behind them might burst open and erupt the mob of greedy relatives into the street.

'What was he doing at the Excelsior offices when the accident happened?'

'That Dodd sent for him. More money wanted, I suppose. It was like pouring it down a drain. I'm sure Dodd stole most of what he got out of Mr. Fallows.'

It was strange that everybody fitted Dodd's behaviour into the same pattern. Thieving, cheating, lying, lechering. He didn't seem to have a friend in the world except Bella Hoop. Remembering what old documents had revealed at Piper's house, Cromwell asked if Fallows had a store of old business papers indoors.

'No, he hadn't. I think he kept them in a box either at the bank or else at the office. I don't know really. He'd nothing here, if what the family say is true. They've been rummaging about like a lot of hungry ferrets. There's nothing come to light except two or three premium bonds, his savings bank book with four pounds, nine and fivepence in it, and next week's football pools forms. Some people take to drink when they've lost all they had, others take to the pools.'

These were the men who had been directors of a company and had tried without success to run it. No wonder it had failed and Dodd had had all his own way about matters.

'Perhaps he kept some papers with him in his pocket-book?'

'The police have taken that. Harry has been to the police station enquiring about that already and they sent him off with a flea in his ear. Harry's the one who was once a boxer. Battling Fallows, he called himself... *Hé!*'

The single exclamation expressed quite a lot.

There seemed little else to ask.

'Did Mr. Fallows say what Mr. Dodd wanted him for?'

'No. But I guessed. The usual.'

Cromwell was now eager to get back to the police station and examine the wallet taken from Fallows's dead body. Not that he expected to find much. If there had been any clues, the local police would have told him. So, he bade Mrs. Henniker good-day.

'You'll have a lot to do, Mrs. Henniker...'

'As soon as the funeral's over, I'm going to my sister's at Sittingbourne and leaving the lot of them to take the place apart and fight over any money that's left. Good-day to you.'

She quickly threw back the door to reveal a knot of listening relations, caught in the act, and now trying to look as if they were innocent. That was the last Cromwell saw of them and he wasn't sorry. Battling Fallows called something after him, but he hurried on without even turning round.

The charred clothes of the dead men had been removed and deposited at the police station. Fallows must, somehow, have been farther away from the explosion and fire than the other two. His suit was hardly damaged, although badly stained, and his wallet was intact, lying on the desk with his money, keys, pipe, watch and other trifles from the pockets. The police had examined the wallet and listed the contents, but Cromwell opened it again and turned out the enclosures on the table.

Nothing out of the ordinary. Two pounds ten in notes; a trade union membership card; a snapshot of a man and woman in what must have been holiday clothes with a background of the sea...

'That was Fallows and his wife,' said a constable who had been breathing down Cromwell's neck as he worked.

A few more odds and ends. Stamps, Excelsior trade cards, a receipt from the local savings bank for a 'sealed envelope marked "will"'.

So that was where it was.

Fallows had been particularly short of all financial and sentimental ties if his private papers were anything to go by and seemed to have been living on the edge of poverty thanks to the claims of Excelsior.

There were ample reasons on every hand for the murder of Dodd; but not for those of Fallows and Piper.

There was one other item. A small envelope with *Excelsior Joinery Co. Ltd.* printed on the flap. It had been unused and there were one or two pencil words on it.

'He was holding that in his hand when we came to examine the body at the mortuary. He must have been writing on it and have clutched it sort of convulsively, like, when the explosion happened.'

Cromwell looked at the writing. An illiterate scrawl, but legible. Fallows must have been making notes in pencil.

> *O/d......... 4100*
> *Takeover £5,000*
> *Loans 1800...... 10/- in the pound.*
> *Polydore I & P.*

'I'd like to take this with me, if you please.'

The policeman looked surprised.

'I can't make head or tail of it. It says something about a takeover. Who'd want to take over a bankrupt business like the Excelsior?'

'We'll have to find out, won't we?' said Cromwell and he put the envelope carefully in his black notebook.

'Where would I be likely to find Mrs. Dodd? She was at the seaside, I hear, when Dodd met his death. I suppose she came home.'

'She came back, but I don't know where she is at present. Her father is Alderman Vintner, a would-be big-shot of the town and a member of the council watch committee. So you'd better be careful. I can't think Mrs. Dodd would go back to her father's place. He quarrelled with Dodd and, from what I hear, cut off Mrs. Dodd with a shilling because she came down on Dodd's side.'

'Where is the Dodds' home?'

'They moved not long ago to a bungalow in Strathallan Road, in the new town. I don't know where they got the money from, but they did. It seemed funny to everybody at the time, Dodd buying a new house and the Excelsior nearly bust.'

'I'll be off to Strathallan Road, then. How do I find it?'

The bobby conducted Cromwell to a large map of the neighbourhood which covered one wall of the charge room and laboriously gave him directions.

It was raining hard outside and Cromwell borrowed a police car; the driver took him straight to the Dodds' new house. It stood in a long road of new property, with houses springing up like mushrooms. Rows and rows of them and excavations still going on. Water the colour of milky tea poured from the new sites, along the gutters of the road, and vanished down the grilles. There was hardly anyone about. The builders' men had fled for shelter from the rain and were drinking tea in half-erected properties.

Cromwell turned in at the gate of Dodd's bungalow. He winced at the name. *Dunromin*. It somehow sounded like Dodd. It was one of the better type on the estate, standing in about half an acre of land, and the front garden was only half turned over.

A woman passed with an umbrella raised and a dog dragging along on a tight rein.

'There's nobody at home,' she said.

Cromwell wondered how she knew, but hurried along the asphalt drive and rang the bell. There was a peal of bells behind the door. But no answer. The inquisitive woman with the half-choked dog was waiting for him.

'Didn't I tell you there was nobody at home...'

And she went on without another word, obviously satisfied at having won the rubber.

'Now what?'

The driver of the police car asked the question rhetorically, for he knew his advice would be asked.

'I might say the same to you.'

'She might have made it up with her dad, now that Dodd's dead. Like to try?'

'Where does Alderman Vintner live?'

'You'll never guess. In a new road not far from here. It's called Vintner Avenue. Named after him. A continuation of the council estate, the new streets of which were called after the reigning aldermen. That is, all except Alderman Drain and Alderman Bastard. The streets luckily gave out before their turns came.'

'Vintner Avenue, then. What's the name of the house? *Chez nous?*'

'No. *Tudor Nook...*'

They found it easily. It was twice as large and twice as ostentatious as any house in sight. Olde Englyshe style, with a garage for four or five cars. The newly planted trees were dripping with rain and the flower-beds in the sodden lawns were a mash of black earth and clay. Cromwell sought the bell-push under the huge porch. Another peal of bells sounded indoors. An elderly housekeeper answered. She looked hard at Cromwell.

'Is Mrs. Dodd at home?'

'You from the undertakers? Because…'

'Police.'

'She won't see you. She's not seeing anybody.'

A voice from inside said 'who is it?' and Mrs. Dodd appeared to find out for herself.

'I'm Mrs. Dodd. What can I do for you?'

'I'm from the police, Mrs. Dodd, and I wonder if you could spare me a minute.'

'You'd better come inside instead of standing in the rain…'

She led him through a large hall. There were two snarling tiger-skins rugs on the polished floor, primitive weapons hung on the walls, which were panelled in dark oak. On one panel hung a large portrait in oils of Alderman Vintner in his alderman's livery, or whatever it was…

'Come in the morning-room.'

The room was small and comfortable. There was a refinement about it which, at first, puzzled Cromwell. After the disorderly array in the hall, the ferocity and bad taste spread about there, this quiet little place seemed incongruous, a spot apart and free from the aggressive domination of whoever had built and furnished the house. There was a portrait of a woman with a dark, gentle oval face over the fireplace which caught Cromwell's eye as soon as he entered the room.

'It is my mother. She is dead.'

Mrs. Dodd, perhaps feeling his interest and answering an unasked question, as though it were of some importance. To

Cromwell it certainly explained much. The mixture of taste and vulgarity in the house, and the personality of Mrs. Dodd herself. She was a mixture of the picture in the hall of her father and that of her mother. Her dark features and oval face were those of one; the sensual mouth and arrogant, rebellious eyes and manner were those of the other. It perhaps accounted for her attraction to Dodd, her quarrel with her father, and her lack of any signs of grief at the tragedy in her life.

Cromwell found it difficult to explain his visit.

'I called at your own home, but found it empty, so thought I'd see if you were staying with your father...'

It sounded a fatuous introduction and she seemed to think so, too.

'I am staying with him for the time being. I suppose the police know that we didn't get on very well together. My father invited me back here... What has that to do with the police? How does it concern you?'

'It isn't really any business of ours, Mrs. Dodd. I'm sorry to intrude at a time like this, but there are one or two matters I'd like to talk over with you if you feel so disposed. You know this is murder and the sooner we settle certain problems, the sooner we hope to find out who committed the crime.'

'I can't help you. I suppose it is known to the police that my husband and I quarrelled before his death. I had left him and was with the children with friends in Wales. The children are still there and I am here. Is there anything else?'

She sat down as though she was sure that wasn't the end of it, and irritably told Cromwell to take a chair, too.

'You will probably have found out why my husband and I disagreed. If you haven't, I don't propose to tell you.'

'I hadn't called to delve into your private affairs, madam. Just to ask you one or two questions about your late husband. First, had he any enemies?'

Her face was stony and as she spoke, showed no signs of her feelings. The room overlooked the back garden and a gardener in a raincoat with a sack round his shoulders was working in the rain, banking up a row of brussels sprouts.

'Enemies? Quite a lot, I would think. Anyone with money invested in that wretched joinery company, for example, would hate his guts. But not enough to kill him. None of them had courage enough to do that.'

'Who *would* have courage?'

'I don't know and if I did I wouldn't tell. It's not up to me to put the rope round anyone's neck. That's the work of the police.'

'Your father disliked him?'

'Incompatibility of temperament, shall we say. Beyond that, I will say no more. If you called to try to get me to incriminate my father, you had better go.'

She answered everything in an indignant voice, as though resenting his presence, yet eager to know what the police were doing in the case.

'Have you found out anything which will lead to an arrest?'

Her self-possession was wonderful. The only evidence of any tension at all was the occasional biting of her under-lip.

'No. The whole affair is a complete mystery. What was he doing there at that hour and why were the two other directors there with him?'

'He didn't confide in me about his business affairs. I was away from home, as I told you, when the office was blown up and I'd no idea how or why it happened.'

She was obviously a hostile witness, embittered with Dodd and all connected with him, probably through his affair with Fred Hoop's wife. That was a matter Cromwell daren't raise at the moment for fear of another explosion.

He rose to go.

'Did he ever mention the word *Polydore* in the course of conversation?'

For the first time, she registered some feeling, but only briefly. Her eyelids flickered and Cromwell knew the shot had gone home.

'No. What's the idea...? Polydore? Who's Polydore?'

'It's something which has cropped up in the course of our investigations, a word written on a scrap of charred paper. It may be nothing.'

'It sounds silly to me. What is it? The name of a game? Or a man's name? In any case, I never heard it before.'

Cromwell gave it up.

'I'm very sorry to have troubled you, Mrs. Dodd, and thank you for receiving me so kindly at a time like this. I...'

Someone was inserting a key in the front door, which was violently flung open. A large man struggled to pull down his umbrella and as he did so, spotted Cromwell in the hall. This made his performance with the umbrella much more difficult and increased his anger. He finally succeeded and flung the object from him in a corner of the porch.

A large, heavy man with a square red face, who first groped in the hatstand for a stick, for he was lame, and then made for Cromwell like a bull at a gate.

'You're the man who's arrived in the police car standing at the gate, aren't you? Well, get back in it and be off with you. But first tell me what's the meaning of this impertinence. Calling at my house when I'm out. I'm on the watch committee and someone's going to answer for this.'

He turned to his daughter who was standing at the door of the morning room, apparently enjoying this show of temper.

'Has he been bullying you in my absence? What's he been up to?'

He stood between Cromwell and the door as though about to use his stick on him if he found cause for it.

'This is Inspector Cromwell, father...'

'I don't want to know who he is. I want to know what he's been doing here. What's he after?'

'He came to ask a few questions about John, father, and he's been very polite about it. So you needn't lose your temper and be rude to him. He's just going.'

'I can see that. The sooner the better.'

He turned to Cromwell.

'What need had you to call here with your inquisition? Anything you wanted to know about me or mine, you could have obtained by calling on me at my place of business. It's a liberty to come to my home with your questions. A liberty you'll pay for when I see the Chief Constable...'

Cromwell was rattled.

'I'm sorry if I've disturbed you, Mr. Alderman. If you wish, I'll call at your shop and explain what it's all about. I wouldn't take the liberty of discussing it any further under your own roof.'

'Don't be impertinent. You've done quite enough...'

Mrs. Dodd seemed used to her father's tantrums and was waiting for the storm to die down.

'And now, Mr. Alderman, if you'll kindly stand away from the door, I'll be on my way. I'm sorry to have troubled you, although it was your daughter and not you I called to see.'

Through the open door, Cromwell could see the police car, standing beside the alderman's own, with the driver looking anxiously through the window, half expecting the alderman to throw Cromwell out, neck and crop.

A few sodden passers-by halted in their steps at the loud sounds of the alderman's fury, surprised at a brawl in such an austere neighbourhood.

Mrs. Dodd suddenly interposed, almost casually, as her father paused for breath.

'The Inspector was asking if I knew the name *Polydore*. I said I didn't...'

There was a silence. The alderman was breathing heavily, almost snorting.

'What's that?'

'*Polydore*. The name's cropped up in the case.'

Vintner changed colour. Pale, and then redder than ever. His voice grew husky.

'Here, young man, what's all this about? I want to know what you've been questioning my daughter about...'

'I'll go fully into all that at the police station, if you care to call, sir. Or I could call on you at the shop, as you object to my asking questions here. Good-day, sir.'

And he left Vintner standing gasping on the threshold, like a landed fish, and hurried through the rain to the car.

9

TAKEOVER

LITTLEJOHN AND CROMWELL MET LATE IN THE AFTERNOON of their busy day of working apart and called at Scotland Yard on their way home to discuss the results of their enquiries.

To supplement their information, they also had the report of the experts who had examined the wrecked Excelsior offices, the debris and the bodies of the victims.

No trace of a time-device to explode the dynamite had been found. The explosive had been in the form of blasting sticks, probably two of them. It was, therefore, assumed that it had been fired by a simple ignited fuse. This would avoid the complications of electrical detonation and enable the murderer to take to his heels at once after igniting his petard.

As far as reconstruction went, it was deduced that the victims had been seated at a table in the main office; Dodd and Piper together, Fallows at some distance away from them.

Beneath the offices was a cellar, once used as a storeroom and accessible by an outer door reached by a flight of stone steps from ground level. This door, usually kept locked, had been rescued in a badly charred and battered condition at some distance from the rest of the wreckage. There was a key in the outside of the lock. It seemed certain therefore, that the murderer had planted the dynamite in the cellar under the main office, locked the cellar door and left the key behind, perhaps where he'd found it.

The full force of the explosion had been centred beneath where Dodd and Piper had been sitting. The heavy table had been blown over on top of Fallows and killed him by a crushing blow on the head. Dodd and Piper had been rendered unconscious or killed outright by the blast; in the former event, fire had finished the job.

The papers the group of men might have been studying were charred and beaten out of recognition. The fire had severely damaged the clothes of Dodd and Piper and the contents of their pockets had been reduced to dust.

On the other hand, the papers in Fallows's pockets had been saved by the heavy table, but seemed to include nothing of importance in the case. The only item of any great interest was the envelope clutched in his hand, protected by his body. This had been used for noting down matters probably under discussion at the time of the explosion.

Cromwell passed the envelope to Littlejohn.

'I thought I'd better bring it with me. You know more about company finance than I do. It may be clearer to you than to me, sir.'

'You flatter me.'

Littlejohn examined the envelope.

'O/D... 4,100... That's plain enough. The Excelsior were overdrawn at the bank by that amount at the time, although, it seems, cheques had been issued which would take them over £5,000.

'It's the next item that seems silly to me, however. Takeover 5,000. Surely nobody would make a takeover bid for Excelsior. It's bust and not worth taking as a gift, to say nothing of five thousand pounds.'

'I agree with you. It's not worth having as a gift. We'd do with some financial advice, Cromwell. The Fraud Squad might be able to help. Flight's on holiday. We'll talk to Newell, if he's still here.'

Superintendent Flight of the Fraud Squad was a financial wizard
and the terror of all fiddlers, absconders, dishonest company directors and confidence tricksters everywhere. It was like him to go
for his holidays in November. He couldn't bear hot weather. His
colleague, Inspector Newell, was a suitable supplement to Flight.
He loved heat and couldn't stand the cold. He went to sweltering
overseas resorts every August and indulged in sun-bathing, surf-riding
and fishing for monsters. Flight was at present in Switzerland, high
up in the mountain, revelling in the cold. They made a good pair.
Newell was a chartered accountant; Flight an ex-inspector of taxes.

Littlejohn rang through for Newell, who sounded full of a cold
at the other end of the line.

'I'll come over.'

Which took about ten minutes as he traversed long corridors
and descended flights of stairs.

'It's cold in here. Haven't you turned on the heat?'

Then he greeted them politely.

A tall, nonchalant angular man, impeccably dressed and with
a pleasant round face and pale blue eyes which had a frozen
look which terrified his unwilling clients right from the start. He
sneezed and blew his nose as he sat down, carefully pulling up his
well-pressed trousers.

'We need your help in a case we're on, if you don't mind,
Newell. A case in which we're turning on the heat, as you put it.'

'Delighted. Tell me about it.'

He vigorously rubbed his hands together, either out of eagerness or cold. Then he rose and turned on the electric fire.

'Hope you don't mind. If Flight hadn't been away seeking the
cold, I'd have been in South Africa seeking the heat. This weather's
killing me. Please go on.'

Then Littlejohn outlined the business, brief history and financial position of Excelsior Joinery Company.

They showed him the envelope first.

Newell stared – stupidly, Cromwell later said – at the envelope and pencil notes made on it by Fallows. 'O.D. That's obvious. Short for overdraft.'

Littlejohn and Cromwell could have told him that!

'Takeover. That's more of a problem. What did Excelsior have to take over? A decaying business, a lot of debts, some very dubious assets in the shape of machinery and a stock of timber. Perhaps, on the other hand, they'd a few debts to collect…'

Newell might have been thinking aloud, but to Littlejohn his thoughts weren't very helpful or inspiring. He was sorry Superintendent Flight was away. Flight had a knack of putting his finger in the sore spots of a case with unerring speed.

'Let's assume they *were* taken over for some reason. Accumulated losses, for example, which the company taking-over could claim back from the income tax people. With £5,000 Excelsior could pay off the bank loan and have £900 left. They borrowed £1,800 in loans from directors and friends. The £900 would repay ten shillings in the pound on the loans. But… But… Excelsior must have had a lot of creditors, who'd be on the doorstep clamouring for their share of the money, as well. They'd hardly see the bank and the loanholders liberally helping themselves without wanting their cut as well…'

Obvious! Cromwell was showing signs of impatience at Newell's banal analysis. He thrust his hand in his pocket for his cigarettes, remembered that his doctor had persuaded him to give up smoking, and withdrew it sadly.

'If the directors were arranging a takeover which would rid

them of all the worries of Excelsior, who'd want to blow them sky-high...?' he said irritably.

'Wait. Wait. You're breaking my train of thought... It's this take-over which might give us a clue. Who was taking over and why?'

He looked at Littlejohn and Cromwell as though either or both of them had the answer pat and were holding out on him.

'Polydore I. & P. Whatever that might mean.'

Newell looked annoyed at Cromwell for thus producing a rabbit from the financial hat prematurely.

'Exactly. Why were Polydore interested?'

'Who is Polydore? What is she?'

'Don't be frivolous, Cromwell. I. & P. probably means Investment and Property Company.'

'Have you heard of them before?'

'The name rings a bell. May I use your intercom., Superintendent?'

He rang up his office in distant parts and told Constable Williams to search the files for Polydore and bring the information.

'If it's a property and investment company, they're hardly likely to invest in a tumbledown ruin like the Excelsior. There must be something else. The site! The site and buildings. That'll be it.'

'Those are rented from the former owner's daughters, who inherited the freehold from him.'

Newell looked crestfallen.

'Had Excelsior a lease or option to purchase?'

'I don't know. I'm not a financial wizard. You're the Fraud Squad, not me.'

Cromwell was out of his depth, too. Littlejohn, sitting smoking and silently amused at the duet going on between Cromwell and Newell, thought he'd better interfere.

'We'll find out.'

He took up the 'phone.

'Look up the Bournemouth telephone directory, will you, please, and see if some Misses Jonas are there? I've forgotten their initials, but it's an uncommon name and shouldn't be hard to trace.'

The answer came almost right away, just as Constable Williams arrived. A good-looking, blonde, buxom girl, with a file tucked under her arm. She smiled at Cromwell, who shed his irritability right away. He glanced across at Littlejohn, who was talking to the telephone operator, as though surprised at his continuing to practise humdrum routine with such a Juno there to minister to them.

'There is a Miss Jonas? Right. Please get her for me.'

'Hullo, Miss Williams...'

Littlejohn knew her well. Her hobby was breeding cocker spaniels in kennels at Clapham and last year she'd won the Littlejohn Cup for the best bitch in the Metropolitan Police Dog Show.

She had a file on Polydore. It was an old one which had fallen in the hands of the Fraud Squad when the secretary had misappropriated some of the trust's fund instead of paying them over to the Commissioners of Inland Revenue.

'We've had nothing on it since 1952. The secretary apparently paid up and the case was dropped.'

'Where did he get the money from, Miss Williams?'

'I don't know, Inspector Cromwell. I was too young to know anything about such things at that time.'

Newell did not smile at his assistant's humour. He never laughed or saw a joke. Fraud had taken all the fun out of life for him.

'Never mind that. What's happening to Polydore now? That's what we want to know.'

'There's a note here, sir, presumably made when the files were gone through and cleaned up. "Moribund. Assets realised". It seems to be a dead company with nothing in it.'

'That was when?'

'The note is dated 1953. The directors must have packed up and divided the assets after the secretary defaulted.'

'What were their names?'

'A family, by the looks of it… Henry, Arthur, Eva and Agnes Jonas.'

'What!'

Cromwell looked at Littlejohn to see how he was taking it. The Superintendent had been lighting his pipe and continued to do so until it was going to his satisfaction. Then he took up the telephone.

'Cancel the call to Bournemouth, please.'

'There was no reply, sir.'

'So much the better. Thanks.'

'We'll call at Bournemouth on our way to Evingden in the morning, Cromwell.'

Newell took out his handkerchief and sneezed heavily.

'I hope it's warmer there than here. Will there be anything more? I'm starved to death in this cold room.'

Constable Williams shrugged her powerful shoulders gently. The place was like an oven.

'You might enquire if Polydore has been revived since your last note. I take it, a moribund company can start to flourish again under the right treatment.'

'Yes, it could be bought for an old song and revived. A few pence a share and the thing's done. It'll be a private company, though. Not as easy as a public one, you know.'

Littlejohn smiled at Newell.

'Not to you, surely, Newell. You have your methods, I take it.'

'We have. And you needn't smile about them, sir. They're perfectly straightforward and above board, I can assure you.'

It was Constable Williams's turn to smile, disarmingly, as though confirming her boss's statement. Newell didn't appreciate it.

'That will be all thanks, Miss Williams. You may go.'

'Goodbye and thank you, Miss Williams. How are the dogs getting along?'

'Fine, sir. We'll be keeping the cup, I hope, at the next show.'

'Cup? Show? What's going on?'

Nobody enlightened Newell, who didn't seem to mind. He was very engrossed in his daily duties and was already mentally on the trail of Polydore.

It was sunny in Bournemouth when Littlejohn and Cromwell arrived there next morning. People were strolling along the promenade enjoying the weather and, in odd corners, protected from the breeze, some were sitting reading their newspapers.

The Misses Jonas lived in a cosy, ground-floor flat in a huge block overlooking the Isle of Wight. Littlejohn had telephoned earlier in the day to make sure of a favourable reception and had been most cordially invited to call whenever he liked.

Both Miss Agnes and Miss Eva Jonas met Littlejohn and Cromwell in the small vestibule of their flat. They were a pleasant pair and one was as different from the other as chalk from cheese. Miss Eva, who was small, slim and grey-haired and looked to be well in her fifties, played the piano very well and, in her time, had been a well-known accompanist. Miss Agnes, large and benevolent, with her auburn hair obviously skilfully dyed, for she was reputed to be only two years younger than Miss Eva, had been a prominent contralto in her heyday, and the overall physical development for such a reputation had increased her size to twice that of her sister and given her twice the volume of sound into the bargain.

The two ladies, eminently qualified for the now out-of-date title of gentlewomen, shook hands and immediately started a round of hospitality by leading their visitors to their magnificent drawing-room for coffee and chocolate cake, to which Miss Agnes did full justice as the time went on.

A large, light, airy room, with views of the sea on two sides and the Isle of Wight included in the other. It was furnished in contemporary style, with plenty of colour about. The antiques and Victorian knick-knacks of the old Jonas home near the factory in Evingden had obviously been shed somewhere on the way to Bournemouth. Miss Agnes, in the course of explaining their decorations, gave reasons for their tastes.

'Our dear father taught us never to be sentimental about the past. "Never live in the past," he would tell us. "The present and the future are yours. Regrets for the past and sentiment over its accumulated rubbish, can only bring sorrow." He taught us that, didn't he, Eva, and we have found wisdom in it?'

There were, none the less, accumulated on the walls innumerable relics of departed pleasures. Portraits of famous singers whom Miss Eva must have accompanied and others showing Miss Agnes, then much younger and shapelier, appearing in *Tosca, Rigoletto, La Bohème, Aïda* and other rôles which Littlejohn failed to identify and at which Cromwell struggled to conceal his amusement. There were no signs of instruments or singing about the present room and, scenting Littlejohn's interest in their affairs, Miss Eva, in her gentle cultured way, gave the reason.

'*Live* music is not allowed in the flats. There was once here a Mr. Ludwig, who played the oboe so beautifully and frequently that it cast a cloud of melancholy over the whole building. Now only radio and television are tolerated in reason. Happily, in the grounds of this place, was an old bellevue belonging to the house which was demolished to make place for the flats. We persuaded the owners to retain the summer-house, which was a roomy one, as our studio and we rent it and enjoy our music there without causing a disturbance.'

She then passed what was left of the cake after the inroads by Miss Agnes and her sister poured the tea.

Dominating the room was a huge oil painting of Mr. Henry Jonas in the red robes and befeathered hat of Mayor of the ancient borough of Evingden. The regalia was the same as that worn by Alderman Vintner in the similar picture in his own home, although Vintner carried it with much less dignity and flair. Littlejohn recognised Mr. Jonas from first acquaintance with him in the snapshot recently shown to him of the group taken at the works' outing of long ago. The same torpedo beard, bright eyes, air of gentlemanly ease and the Captain Kettleish humour and confidence.

The expensive flat, the mode of life, the cultured grace and the social standing of Henry Jonas and his two girls must at one time have had their roots in the now tottering Excelsior Joinery Company. At some time or other, it must have yielded abundant profits.

Both ladies, forewarned by Littlejohn of the purpose of his visit, seemed quite unexcited by the sensational happenings in their old hometown.

'We've been so long away and everything there has changed so much. We feel now that we never really belonged there at all. There is, of course, the property which we own and our dear father's and our mother's grave in St. Michael's churchyard, but the town itself has ceased to exist as we knew it.'

'The property is really what concerns us quite a lot in our investigations, Miss Agnes. You still own the freehold?'

'Yes, of course, although we may just as well not do so now. We haven't received any rent for it for the past two... or is it three years, my dear...?'

She made a gesture in the direction of her sister.

'Eva looks after our finances. I was never any good in money matters except in extravagant spending. My sister, on the other hand, has quite a flair and considerably augments our income by fortunate investments on the Stock Exchange.'

Miss Eva made little signs and noises, intended to indicate that this talent was a mere nothing. She was quick to answer the financial enquiry, though.

'We haven't had any rent for three years. The company, whose name was changed to the ridiculous Excelsior title after we sold it, has made a series of losses in recent years. We didn't take any steps to recover the arrears of rent. Our dear father would not have wished us to pursue old servants of the firm who took it over from us.'

'All except that awful Dodd,' interjected Miss Agnes.

'All except Dodd, as you say.'

'Why the dislike of Dodd, Miss Eva?'

'We ought not to speak ill of the dead, but he was a rogue. Our dear father was adept at finance and during his lifetime always made the company pay profits. When Dodd took charge, however, they always made losses.'

'I wouldn't say that was roguery, would you?'

'There are other things...'

Miss Eva hesitated.

'I don't wish to speak ill of the dead, as I said before.'

'In the circumstances, I think you'd better tell us all you know. It will probably help us find whoever killed the three men.'

'In the First World War, Dodd's father was my father's servant, batman, as they call them. My father was an officer in the territorials in those days and he owed his life to Dodd, senior, who went into no-man's land and rescued him as he lay there wounded in the leg. Dodd's father was later killed and my father felt responsible for young Dodd and found him work at the company, where he rose to be confidential secretary. He was not like his father; there was a streak of weakness in his character, perhaps derived from his mother. Dodd was placed in the company office and there did private and family work for father, as well as the company's business.'

Miss Agnes thereupon produced a box of Havana cigars and gave Littlejohn and Cromwell one apiece.

'Excuse my interrupting, but I'm sure you smoke. The smell of a good cigar always reminds us of our dear father. These cigars were some he left behind...'

Years ago! Yet, they'd been well kept and preserved. Littlejohn and Cromwell carefully cut and lighted them, Cromwell, who'd forsworn smoking, mentally excusing himself for a brief lapse. It was like a rite in memory of the dead. The smoke rose like incense and there was a short pause as the spirit of Mr. Henry Jonas pervaded the air.

'To resume, Superintendent. Over a number of years, John Dodd manipulated the books of the Jonas family trust. He appropriated funds for his own use. Quite a substantial sum. More than a thousand pounds. He didn't pay the income tax when it fell due and suppressed letters sent demanding it by the Inland Revenue.

A police case was only avoided by my dear father's intervention. For the sake of Dodd's father, our father paid the thousand pounds out of his own pocket, plus a penalty of £2,000 for submitting improper returns...'

That perhaps explained the record of Polydore Trust in the Fraud Squad files!

'What was the name of your family trust?'

'Polydore Trust Limited. My grandfather who founded the fund for the benefit of his children, was called Henry Polydore Jonas. It was named after him. After Dodd's disgraceful behaviour, we abandoned the use of the trust. It was no longer needed in any case.'

'Did the trust company remain in being?'

'Yes. There were no investments or other assets in it, but the company remained and eventually, strange to say, it was sold.'

'To whom?'

'I will explain. My father actually forgave Dodd. As I told you, he felt he owed it to Dodd's father. He removed everything financial from Dodd's care and gave him the post as traveller, "on the road", as the saying goes. Had father cared to do so, he could have prosecuted Dodd and only with great difficulty prevented the Inland Revenue people from doing so.'

'How did Polydore come to be sold?'

'Our banker approached us and suggested it. Although it was an empty shell, he said he knew some London people who were seeking a moribund company in which to place certain reserve funds. They offered us a nominal sum for the company. Two hundred and fifty pounds for what to us were shares not worth two hundred and fifty pence. Our banker said it would be perfectly legal and, as the name of Jonas did not appear in the title, we felt we could accept the offer without fear. The parties making the offer were said to be very reputable...'

'By whom?'

'Our solicitor and our banker both made enquiries and assured us of the integrity of the people.'

'May I ask the names of the lawyer and bank manager?'

'Of course. Mr. Christopher Boycott, was, and still is, our lawyer and Mr. Handel Roper, of the Home Counties Bank in Evingden, was our banker at the time. Both men of repute.'

Littlejohn wondered!

'Two hundred and fifty pounds for nothing. We decided to accept.'

Miss Eva, whom her sister had described as the financial wizard of the pair of them, had evidently known a good thing when she met it.

'What was the name of the purchasers?'

'The Deliverance Investment and Development Trust.'

What a name!

'Who was behind it?'

'I really don't know and I took the word of Mr. Boycott and Mr. Roper for the integrity of those concerned. They said it was a reputable London private banking connection and the good name of our trust would be preserved. They urged us to accept, as the offer was exceptional.'

'These two gentlemen frequently advised you on such matters?'

'In the confusion arising from the sudden tragic death of our dear father everything was upset and Mr. Boycott and Mr. Roper were most kind to us.'

Miss Agnes had now made some more tea and produced another chocolate cake. They sat for a time, watching the sea and the sunshine across the water and the changing colours of the Isle of Wight as the clouds scudded across the sky.

'May I ask if the new Excelsior company took a lease of the property of the works and offices from you?'

'Yes. When the new company, composed of father's old employees, took over, we agreed to a ten years' lease at £200 per annum. It was specially favourable due to sentiment, you see. My father would have been glad to know into whose hands the family business was passing, although he would not much have cared for John William Dodd being a party to it. Neither did we, but there was nothing we could do without injuring the rest. After all, Dodd seemed to have gone straight after father rescued him.'

'The lease will not have much longer to run now.'

'No. Three or four years more. But there was an option for Excelsior to purchase the property outright for £5,000, if they wished to do so before the lease expired.'

So that was it!

It seemed very much as if, at the time he met his death, Dodd was discussing with his co-directors the taking up of the option and the purchase of the Excelsior buildings.

But why? The company was played out and purchase of the buildings would do it no good. Unless the works could be resold to someone who was eager to buy them. Someone who would buy the lease and make use of the option to acquire the works and offices for another purpose. What purpose?

'Do you mind if I use your telephone, Miss Eva? I must speak to Scotland Yard on an important matter.'

Miss Eva, already greatly thrilled by the presence of a famous detective, was almost overcome by the mention of Scotland Yard. She and her sister were great crime readers and the idea of the

Mecca of detectives being in connection, even by telephone for a few minutes, with their home, gave her a topic of proud conversation for the rest of her life.

Littlejohn spoke again to Newell, of the Fraud Squad, and told him briefly most of the information so willingly given by the Misses Jonas.

'I'll get on to it right away. I've never heard of the Deliverance. With a name like that, I'd not have forgotten it if it had crossed my path. It's probably a private limited company, and, as I said before, information about such concerns is a bit harder to come by. However, we have our ways of getting what we want. I've a rough idea what's been going on, though. It sounds like the old trick.'

'Trick? Be a little more forthcoming, Newell.'

'The trick of having a string of companies, in which one company owns another. It's a way of concealing the immediate ownership of the company, although if you go far enough back and patiently ferret, the rabbits are bound to bolt into the open sooner or later.'

'Sounds double-Dutch to me.'

'That's because you're more interested in murders than in other forms of human jiggery-pokery.'

'What about the lease? Can you add to my confusion by explaining that?'

'I can't be sure of anything until I've looked into matters properly. We might be chasing a red herring. However, the fact that Evingden is a new town is quite a good lead.'

'Still talking in riddles?'

'Not at all. Hasn't it dawned on you, Superintendent, that as soon as the matter of a new town was mooted, land values would rise like mad. And, as the new town spreads, land farther afield round the town begins to rise, too. Let's say, the borough of Evingden decides to build a new town hall and the Excelsior site looks to be the very place. The £5,000 option would be mere chicken feed. Buy the site for £5,000 and sell it for £25,000. See what I'm getting at?'

'I'm beginning to see.'

'And, if you were in the inner counsels of the borough authorities, you'd get the news in advance, confidentially. You could hardly go off right away and buy the site in your own name and sell it later at a huge profit, could you? But if you had a company and had carefully hidden your connection with it, well... Bob's your uncle...'

'Have another cigar, Superintendent,' said Miss Eva when he returned from the telephone.

He'd much have preferred his pipe, but when a lady has given you the key to what might be the last door of an investigation, how can you refuse?

'Have you had a recent offer to purchase the lease and option of the Evingden property, Miss Eva?'

'To tell you the truth, we have. Mr. Roper, the bank manager, telephoned the other day about it.'

'What did he say?'

'He said that he had had a tentative approach by a client who wished to purchase the property with a view to commencing another business in it. He added that, as far as he knew, the Excelsior company was not making profits and might be disposed to sell their lease together with the option to purchase the buildings for £5,000. Would we be prepared to agree to that? You see, Superintendent, according to the lease, if Excelsior wished to sell or transfer it in any way, our consent was necessary.'

'What did you tell Mr. Roper, if I may ask?'

'I consulted my sister and we agreed. We have had no rent for some years and thought that the capital sum of £5,000 would be a very favourable change.'

'Thank you very much for all your help, Miss Eva and Miss Agnes.'

'Please do not hesitate to call again if we can help. Or if you are ever again in Bournemouth…'

'Yes; *do* come again,' added Miss Agnes.

Back in Evingden, Littlejohn called at the Town Hall. The Town Clerk, Mr. Tipstaff, was a new and energetic official, eager to see Evingden grow into a large city. He pictured continued development. At least two Members of Parliament, a bishop, a cathedral, a Recorder, a Lord Mayor…

'What can I do for you, Superintendent? I've only a few minutes to spare… Meeting of the General Purposes Committee…'

He was tall and thin and had a long flushed nose and cold washed-out eyes.

'I won't keep you, sir? I just wished to ask you if the Corporation of Evingden propose to develop the site on which the Excelsior joinery works now stands.'

Mr. Tipstaff was seated behind a huge desk littered with documents and large books. He leapt to his feet with gestures and looks of horror.

'Who has told you that, Superintendent?'

'I am on the case of the explosion at the Excelsior works, sir. The information has come to light during the investigation.'

Mr. Tipstaff's cold eyes widened and grew suddenly bright with malice.

'Then you had better put it from your mind. What the corporation plans and does not plan is in no way connected with that case.'

'You must leave me to be the judge of that, sir. I can obtain confirmation of the matter elsewhere if I wish. I ask you because if the information is confidential, you may prefer to help me and tell me it hasn't yet been made public. Then, I will keep the secret.'

'What about your informant?'

'My informant will do the same. I will see to that.'

Mr. Tipstaff was not used to being forced into awkward corners. As a rule, he did the forcing. He looked very angry and undecided.

'Have I your word not to repeat what I may be prepared to tell you?'

'I believe you are a solicitor, sir. As such you are an officer of the court. If you are able to assist us in our enquiries it is your duty to do so. I assure you the information is of great importance in this investigation... please don't interrupt me, sir... It is of importance in this investigation and whatever you may care to tell me will be regarded as confidential by the police. I cannot say more.'

Mr. Tipstaff looked at his watch. It was time for the meeting.

'I'll think it over.'

'This is urgent, sir. If you are not disposed to answer my question, I shall have to enquire elsewhere.'

'Elsewhere! Dammit, man!!'

And then he suddenly gave in.

'Very well. I have your word. The corporation propose to purchase the land for a bus station. That information has not been made public yet. The valuers haven't even fixed the price we propose to offer.'

'It is valuable land, I presume, in view of the extending town.'

'That is right.'

'What might be the purchase price?'

Mr. Tipstaff looked here and there as though seeking a place in which to hide.

'Really! What has that to do with it? As I said, we haven't made an offer yet, in any case.'

'What could such an offer amount to?'

'You are very persistent. What good will it do if I tell you?'

'This. Our investigations have led us to suspect there has, for some years, been a racket going on in this town. Before the new town began to be built, land was being bought by those who knew the future of Evingden, at low prices and later sold at huge profits. These land grabbers knew before anyone else what was going to happen. They cashed in on the confidential information to which they had access…'

'But… Who…?'

'I have now reason to believe the Excelsior works is yet another of their speculations. They can acquire it for £5,000…'

Mr. Tipstaff almost collapsed. He spoke in a broken whisper.

'My own view is that the corporation would have paid up to £15,000.'

'Your confidences will not go out of this room, sir. If this case ends in the way I think it will, you, as lawyer to the council, are going to have a busy time. Thank you for your help, sir. I won't keep you from your meeting. But not a word of this. We don't want to scare the rabbit before we've loaded the gun…'

'Rabbit? Gun?'

He picked up his papers and made for the door as though about to slaughter someone in the forthcoming meeting.

'Who is it?'

'All in good time, sir.'

Mr. Tipstaff was a changed man. He seemed to want a friend. He clutched Littlejohn's hand with his cold fingers and shook it.

'I am depending on you, Superintendent… Rabbit… Gun…'

He bared his teeth in a mirthless smile.

'It will be a pleasure to see you pull the trigger… Don't be long.'

He pumped Littlejohn's arm up and down again and then left him to usher himself out.

Cromwell was waiting in the car outside the massive new town hall. He grinned.

'Get what you want, sir?'

'Not half!'

Suddenly Tattersall rushed from the adjacent police station. He almost ran to the car, maintaining his dignity with difficulty.

'The very man I want to see. Another victim.'

'Who is it this time?'

'Handel Roper. About an hour ago, he received a telephone call from Miss Eva Jonas, of Bournemouth. He at once took out his car, went down to Brighton, and threw himself off the pier. He's dead.'

POOK'S RETREAT

MISS EVA JONAS SOUNDED VERY SURPRISED WHEN LITTLEJOHN asked her over the telephone about her conversation with Handel Roper.

'But I only asked him if the sale of the lease was likely to take place. I told him you had been with us and enquiring about it and that I had mentioned that he had a client who was a likely purchaser.'

And Roper had immediately made off to Brighton and drowned himself!

It was just after one o'clock when the news of Roper's suicide reached Evingden. It was at once passed on to the Home Counties Head Office in London, and before three, the bank inspectors arrived. In view of the gravity of the situation and the fact that Scotland Yard were involved, the bank's Chief Inspector himself led the team of investigators and he was endowed with plenipotentiary authority to deal with Littlejohn. A decent little perky fellow, named Powicke, of whom all the bank staff seemed scared to death, much to his astonishment, and who said he had often heard of Littlejohn from his friend, Superintendent Flight, of the Fraud Squad. He enthusiastically assured Littlejohn of his discreet co-operation.

First of all, the inspectors checked the cash and found it right to a penny. Then they checked all the securities, and, at one o'clock in the morning were able to retire to bed assured that they were all there.

'He evidently hadn't been fiddling the books,' yawned the junior man who carried the official bag and was going to sleep in the

bathroom of an hotel because the number of beds for strangers
had not yet grown with the town.

After the news of Roper's death arrived, Littlejohn spent a
busy afternoon.

His first query drew a blank. It was made over the telephone to
Mr. Christopher Boycott, solicitor, it seemed, to most of the influential people at Evingden. He asked him about the Polydore Trust
and at once sensed that he had trodden on Mr. Boycott's corns.

'Polydore Trust. Yes, I remember it. Why?'

'I was speaking to the Misses Jonas about it this morning.
They told me you recommended that they should sell the shares
to Deliverance Trust. Is that so, sir?'

'Look here! Why this inquisition?'

'Polydore has cropped up in the Excelsior explosion case which
we're investigating.'

'In what way?'

'It's too long a tale to tell over the telephone, sir. I'll call and
explain personally later.'

'In that case, I'll wait until you call before I tell you. Look here,
it's most improper to conduct investigations of that kind over the
telephone.'

'Very well, sir. I was trying to save your time and mine. In any
event, had Mr. Roper been available, I could have obtained the
information from him, and need not have troubled you.'

'Why? Is Roper out of town?'

'He's dead, sir.'

There was an eloquent silence as Boycott recovered his breath.

'Say that again.'

'Mr. Roper died this morning. He was found drowned near
Brighton pier.'

'Suicide?'

'Presumably.'

'My God!'

'You hadn't heard, sir?'

'I've been out of town, too.'

Littlejohn wondered if Mr. Boycott had been contemplating Brighton pier as well.

'Look here, Littlejohn. Have you any idea why this has happened?'

'No, sir. We will have to investigate that, too.'

'Keeping you busy in Evingden, aren't we? Look here...'

Littlejohn was getting fed up with being told to look here, but listened patiently.

'Look here... I'm sorry I was a bit brusque with you. These local tragedies are trying all our nerves. The question you asked me... About Deliverance Trust. Miss Eva Jonas enquired about them. I got the information from Roper. He'd enquired from the information office of his bank in London. That's all I can tell you.'

'Thank you, sir.'

'Any progress in the case?'

'We've collected a lot of information, but, as yet, haven't reached any definite conclusions.'

'I wish you well.'

'Thank you, sir.'

'And look here...'

Again!

'If I can be of any help, don't hesitate.'

'I'm very grateful to you, sir.'

Next, to the new branch of the Home Counties. Mr. Caffrey said he'd just returned from his lunch. When he gave this information,

Littlejohn suddenly realised he and Cromwell hadn't eaten since Miss Agnes had stuffed them with chocolate cake.

'I won't keep you long, Mr. Caffrey...'

'Don't worry. Always at your disposal. Poor old Roper. All this Excelsior trouble coming at a time when he was under the weather, must have been too much for him. It's upset me. I was brought up under Handel Roper, as I said before. He was like a father to me when I was at his office.'

'He wasn't a wealthy man, I gather.'

'No. His wife's extravagant. I'd guess he lived pretty well up to his income. When I was at his branch, he was never flush with funds. He was a generous man, but couldn't afford to be as free as he'd have liked to be.'

'What about Dodd?'

'Badly off. We had to watch his account to see that he didn't overdraw. We bounced his cheques now and then. All this, of course, was nine or ten years ago, but I don't think matters have changed much for the pair of them.'

'Dodd married Alderman Vintner's daughter, didn't he?'

'Yes. I'd left Roper's branch then. The alderman's private and business accounts were there and still are. In the old days, Vintner's business was on its last legs, too. Too many up-to-date plumbers competing with him, and his ironmongery side was old-fashioned. Then came this new town business and Vintner's fortunes seemed to change. He used to live over the shop. Now he has a lavish sort of house in the better part of the town. The new Evingden's been a godsend to Vintner.'

'Well, thank you, Mr. Caffrey. I won't detain you, especially as I've not had my lunch yet...'

Littlejohn hurriedly sought out Cromwell, who was busy at

the police station keeping Tattersall up-to-date about their morning's visits, and took him out to lunch at the *Cat and Fiddle*, a new Evingden pub, humming with life and serving a wide range of dishes and drinks of the types covered by expense accounts.

When, later, the bank inspectors arrived at the Home Counties, Littlejohn had to wait until the amiable Powicke had deployed his men and then they got together in the dark, sad room of Mr. Roper.

'Have you any information, Superintendent, which might give us a lead as to why Roper should wish to take his own life?'

'He seemed depressed about his future, as far as I could gather. Also, I understand that he'd allowed Excelsior a large overdraft, albeit secured, against the wishes of his head office.'

'Did he actually tell you all this?'

'Not in so many words, but from the course of our conversation, I got clear impressions of his state of mind. I would, if you can divulge it, be very glad to learn certain things concerning the case. To explain some of my queries would take a long time. If you'd be patient, I'd tell you all about it later.'

'There's no harm in your asking me what you want to know.'

'From local accounts, I gather that Roper wasn't very well off. Is that so?'

'In confidence, I can say that he wasn't. He seemed to get through all his salary each month. I believe his wife was a great spender. I was afraid when I heard of his suicide that his books might be wrong. But such isn't the case, as far as I've been able to gather from a cursory check.'

'Was he likely to have money tucked away elsewhere?'

'I couldn't say, but it's unlikely. When you entered, I was just about to open his private safe...'

He indicated the modern little safe installed in one corner of the room, and took up a bunch of keys lying on the desk in front of him.

'He alone had the key for that. His body is in the Brighton mortuary at the moment, but the police have sent his keys at our request. He had them in his pocket.'

The safe contained private codes, secret instructions, copies of staff reports and a small strong-box for personal papers. There was nothing unusual there. Powicke went carefully through the loose papers and shook his head.

'This strong-box probably contains his private effects and I really ought to open it in front of his lawyer. Perhaps we might take a look to see if that is so, and then close it without disturbing the contents...'

He selected a small key and gingerly opened the box.

One side of it held what they had expected; a will, life policies, items of jewellery... The other was occupied by a number of pass-books, which disclosed that Mr. Roper had kept an account with a rival bank in the city of London, and also had deposits with three building societies. The total of such funds amounted roughly to over five thousand pounds.

'Well, I'll be damned! I wonder what all this means?'

'We'd perhaps better lock it all up without further investigation, sir, until you can have Mr. Roper's lawyer present. I see from the envelope containing the will that Mr. Boycott drew it up.'

'Yes. I'll get him right away and we'll go into things in more detail then.'

'When you have a chance to examine the various pass-books in the box, Mr. Powicke, would it be possible to trace when he accumulated all that money?'

'I can't say. But we'll try. He must have had some other source of income. He certainly didn't accumulate so much money from savings out of his bank salary. I'll keep in touch with you. Meanwhile, I'll have to get on with my report. I've to post it off to Head Office tonight...'

The telephone on the desk rang. Powicke answered it.

'It's for you, Superintendent.'

It was Newell, of the Fraud Squad, sounding very satisfied with himself.

'Nice warm day, sir, in spite of the rain, isn't it? I've been making enquiries about Deliverance Investment and Development Trust. It is virtually owned by yet another trust. The farther one goes in these matters, the more unlikely the cat is to jump out of the bag. But we've followed the trail. The trust which owns Deliverance is Pook's Retreat Development Company...'

'Good Lord! What in the world's Pook's Retreat? Who owns it? Pook?'

'Not so fast, Superintendent. We've reached bottom. The chain ends with Pook. Pook's Retreat is in Surrey, not far from Dorking. It seems that Mr. Pook was a banker in search of peace. He built himself a nice house on a quiet estate, died a hundred years ago, and left it to his children. Eventually house and grounds passed into the hands of a property developer who seems to have objected to retreats and who formed a company to build houses on it. All of them were sold and the Pook's Retreat company was no longer required for the job. So, it was put to other purposes. With the help of subsidiaries, it began to buy land on spots likely to develop and appreciate.'

'Who owned it?'

'It was formed by a chap of the name of Sandman, Morris Sandman. Are you still listening, Superintendent?'

'I certainly am!'

'He died about six years ago and the company was reorganised. By the way, there were only two directors when the company was founded; now there are five.'

'Who was the original co-director?'

'I'm coming to it. Have you got a piece of paper handy?'

'Yes.'

'Well, I'll give you a complete list. First, founded by Morris Sandman. Co-director, Beatrice Sandman. Secretary, Bella Pochin Sandman...'

'Keeping it in the family, I see. Go on, please.'

'I hope you're duly grateful for all this, Superintendent. It's a jigsaw puzzle assembled with the assistance of half the banks in London. Nothing really confidential, but just a matter of finding the right place in which to ask. Morris Sandman died in 1957. For a little time the Pook's company lay resting. Then it started again with a new board. Chairman, Beatrice Sandman. Directors, Bella Pochin Hoop, John William Dodd, George Frederick Handel Roper and Hartley Roderick Ash. Secretary, Oswald Bugler. Got it?'

'Yes, thank you very much. This will be a great help, though I must confess I don't know which end to start at. I'll let you know how we get along... Goodbye...'

Bella Pochin Hoop! That was a good one!

Mr. Powicke could hardly stop his ears and had been listening to the one-sided conversation with great interest.

'Got onto something, Superintendent?'

'I think so, sir.'

He paused and looked at the list on the old envelope he'd been using. What a motley crew! And what a bag of mystery!

He turned to the expectant bank inspector.

'I think I can guess where some of Roper's monies have come from, at least. He's been in a syndicate speculating in land... and very successfully, too.'

Mr. Powicke threw up his hands.

'Great heavens!'

'As you say, sir, great heavens. I suppose that such an enterprise, coming on top of his routine misdemeanours, would have meant the sack for Mr. Roper if Head Office had found out...'

'It certainly would. It's against the regulations to speculate and Roper, as an official, had signed an undertaking to abjure such conduct.'

'From experience of the affairs of this... this consortium, would you call it?... I don't think you'll find much trace of his connection with it in Mr. Roper's account with your bank. They were accustomed to dealing in cash.'

'And his suicide?'

'Poor Roper was at his wits' end. The explosion and deaths at the Excelsior must have put the fear of God in him. Perhaps he wondered if he'd be the next.'

'They surely weren't going to blow up the bank as well?'

Mr. Powicke paled at the thought.

'Hardly. He wondered what a more or less public enquiry into the catastrophe and the deaths of Dodd and his colleagues would reveal. He was afraid his connection with the syndicate would come out. Then, I asked a perfectly simple question of one of his old customers and she contacted Roper and told him what it was about. You see, he was her banker and she liked to have his advice on money matters. That was the end for Roper. He was sure we were investigating tracks which would lead us to the syndicate and himself. He was faced with ruin. He couldn't bear the disgrace the discovery would bring upon him.'

'Poor Roper. I'll tell you in confidence, too, that on top of his other troubles, the accountant here reports to me, Vintner, one of his most influential customers, recently had a fearful row with Roper and was heard to shout that he would not only remove his own accounts to a rival bank, but use his influence to obtain a transfer of the Evingden Corporation accounts, which are kept at this office, to another bank, as well. Head Office would have regarded such losses with extreme displeasure and wanted full reasons for them.'

'When was that, sir?'

Powicke consulted his notes.

'November 8th, about noon.'

Littlejohn then gave the chief inspector a list of the land companies starting from Pook's Retreat and ending with Polydore.

'If you come across transactions bearing these names, will you please let me know?'

'Certainly. By the way, Roper wasn't involved in the death of the three men in the explosion, was he?'

'I hardly think so. I'm sure he wasn't a killer. He had, of course, motive, but he would never have murdered for it.'

'Motive? What motive?'

'The loan to Excelsior. Head Office of the bank had refused to grant it; yet, in spite of that, Roper allowed it.'

'That is true.'

'Had it ended as a bad debt, Roper's career might have been in great jeopardy. And he'd only a few years more to serve. He'd have lost his pension and his job.'

'I hardly think the bank would have treated him so roughly.

He'd probably have been retired on a smaller pension to get him out of the way.'

'In any case, in his mental state, he doubtless imagined the worst. The security for the loan was definitely bad. Guarantees of directors which weren't worth the paper they were written on and a tumbledown business with nothing behind it except a lot of old machinery worth scrap-iron price. There was only one way that would save Roper. Dodd had deposited in cover for his guarantee for the full amount of the loan, a life policy, worth next to nothing whilst he was alive, but sufficient to repay the loan if he died...'

Mr. Powicke almost stopped breathing.

'And...?'

'Well? The loan will be repaid in full because Dodd *has* died.'

Mr. Powicke, in the course of his duties, had unearthed some queer things in the banking world, but never anything like this.

'Good heavens!' he shouted so loudly, that one of his passing assistants rushed into the room, thinking Littlejohn had attacked him.

BUGLER SCARED

M R. BERT SCRIBOMA LOOKED VERY SURPRISED WHEN LITTLE-john paused at the door of his licensed betting establishment in a flashy first floor office just off the main street.

'I am honoured, Superintendent, by your custom. I saw your picture in yesterday's paper and was glad they'd called you in to clear up the mess at the Excelsior. You're not goin' inside, are you? Because, if you are, I'd better show you the back door. If you entered by the front, the clients might think somethin' was up.'

Bert, small, swarthy and pushing, was dressed in a light suit, pointed shoes, natty Tyrolean hat and his thumbs were thrust through the armholes of his waistcoat. He was smoking a cigar.

'Is your brother-in-law, Mr. Bugler, working for you now?'

Mr. Scriboma's whippet face creased into oily smiles.

'Yes, he is. Ossie's a wizard at figures and was wastin' his time at that dump. He's in the back room. I'll show you.'

It was time, too. A number of customers hurrying to place bets with Bert, turned and scuttered away when they saw Littlejohn standing at the door.

Mr. Scriboma led Littlejohn to the entrance of a small dark corridor, down which he peered first to make sure that nothing fishy was going on.

'First to the right. You'll find Ossie there.'

He was. Sitting in his shirt sleeves grinding out the odds on a second-hand calculating machine which resembled a revolving steel hedgehog. Mr. Bugler looked alarmed.

'Anything wrong?'

It probably expressed his inmost thoughts.

'I want some more help from you, if you don't mind.'

'Not at all.'

He turned to a girl with a fancy hair-do who was sorting slips in a corner.

'Miss Powell. Just take a walk for five minutes and get me a packet of cigarettes.'

Miss Powell gave Ossie a sly look as though sure that something seedy was afoot and left the place without even asking for his money. Bugler then quietly closed the door between the main office and the room he occupied. This cut off the sounds of shuffling, tramping feet and the clink of money, which sounded like an employment exchange on pay day.

'Sit down, sir.'

Bugler took out a battered packet of cigarettes and helped himself to one.

'Do you indulge? I've started smoking again.'

He'd broken out again under the recent strain!

'No, thanks.'

'What can I do for you?'

'Have you ever heard of the business of Pook's Retreat…?'

Bugler didn't wait to hear the rest.

'Pook's Retreat? Who's he?'

But Bugler knew very well. He was a changed man. His sandy hair seemed to rise on end and he looked at the outer door as though ready to make a run for it.

Littlejohn continued like a player flinging out a winning hand at nap.

'Or Deliverance Trust…? Or Polydore Trust…?'

'Stop! I haven't done anything wrong. I was tricked into it.'

'Nobody's saying you have done wrong, Mr. Bugler. I want some information about the companies I've just mentioned.'

'Why pick on me, sir?'

'Because you are the secretary of, at least, one of them. I want to ask you some questions about them.'

'I think I'd better get my lawyer in… This is trust business, confidential…'

'I suppose Mr. Hartley Ash is your lawyer, is he? No need for him. I'm not going to arrest you, Mr. Bugler.'

Mr. Bugler stubbed out his half-smoked cigarette and feverishly lit another.

'If I do help you, you'll see I'm done right by?'

Before Littlejohn could answer Mr. Scriboma strutted in, puffing opulently at his cigar.

'Everythin' O.K.? Eh?'

'Yes, Bert,' lied Mr. Bugler. 'Mind if I talk with this gentleman for a few minutes?'

Mr. Scriboma patted Bugler's narrow shoulders amiably.

'Of course. Take all the time you want, Ossie. Mind if I leave you? Business is brisk…'

They were glad to see him go. Bugler swallowed hard.

'Well?'

'How did you get mixed up in the Pook's Retreat syndicate, Mr. Bugler?'

'It was through John Willie Dodd. He was a member of it. They asked him to be secretary, but he said nothing short of a director would do for him and he wasn't doing any of the book-keeping either. He asked me if I'd like to earn a hundred a year for doing nothing. I saw no harm in it. I did no harm either. I wasn't one of the board. I was just a paid official.'

'How did Dodd get his foot in it?'

Bugler looked ready to weep. His hands trembled and his eyes shifted all over the place.

'I don't know.'

Littlejohn slowly filled his pipe.

'I think we'd better go across to the police station and finish our business there. This place seems disturbing to you...'

'No! For God's sake, not there. If I was to be seen going through the town with you...'

'What are you afraid of?'

'*You* ask *me* that? One director blown to hell in his office. And now another's thrown himself off Brighton pier. I'll be the next if I don't look out.'

'Who are you afraid of?'

'I don't know. If I knew I'd tell you and then you could arrest him. He's the murderer you're after.'

'Calm down. Tell me how Dodd got in the syndicate.'

'Nobody ever told me. I only guessed.'

'It was more than that, wasn't it, Mr. Bugler? As secretary of the companies, didn't you have access to the minute book? Let's begin at the beginning, shall we?'

'Miss Powell will be back any minute...'

'Send her for another packet of cigarettes, then. Well?'

Bugler licked his lips and mopped his forehead with a soiled handkerchief.

'Where do I begin?'

'Pook's Retreat.'

'It was an old company formed by Morris Sandman for building development. Then he used it for land purchases in this district.'

'But not directly.'

'I see what you mean. No. The name was known locally through Sandman, you see, so they took over other companies which weren't so well known or wouldn't attract attention or suspicion. Is that all?'

'You know it isn't. As soon as there was a whisper about Evingden becoming a large overspill town, land prices rose phenomenally, but before the whisper got around, the directors of the syndicate had already bought heavily.'

'That's right.'

'The first board of Pook's Retreat consisted of just Sandman, his wife and his daughter. Then more members were added. Dodd and Hartley Ash.'

'Hartley Ash was just the lawyer…'

'Also Mr. Roper from the bank joined you.'

'Financial adviser. He was brought in to arrange and advise about loans to purchase properties…'

'Not through his own bank, though.'

'Of course not. They wouldn't have played. Besides, this was hush-hush. If it had got out about the new town, land would have gone up sky-high.'

'Where did the finance come from, then?'

'Mr. Roper had friends in London. Private banks and mortgage companies. He arranged things that way.'

'Why was Dodd in it? He wasn't expert in anything, was he?'

'I suppose they thought he knew about building construction and the like, being the main man at Excelsior…'

'Come, come, Mr. Bugler. That won't do. They didn't propose to *develop* land. They bought it to sell again at huge profits to those who wanted it for development.'

Bugler scuttered to one corner and back, like a rat in a trap. Then he faced Littlejohn and thrust out his hands in despair.

'I told you. It's as much as my life's worth to talk. Look at what's happened to Dodd and Roper. Don't push me, or I might end up like Roper. I can't stand it.'

'The police are in this now, Mr. Bugler. We'll see that no harm comes to you.'

Bugler seemed to make up his mind and told his tale to Littlejohn in a low voice, like a chant, a *miserere*, punctuated by apologies and excuses.

'It started in a small way. Sandman bought properties locally, before anything was said about the new town. He had a flair for speculation. Then, he must have got wind about the new town and wanted some fuller information, so that he could buy sites which would be most in demand. He got hold of Alderman Vintner...'

It was coming out now!

Bugler seized Littlejohn by the lapels of his coat.

'You won't say a word about this that will put me in danger. If it got out that I'd...'

'I said we'd protect you. Go on.'

'Vintner was on the small private committee of the Evingden Council which arranged about the new town. He knew all the plans and where the main buildings and developments would be sited. The very man for Sandman. He picked the spots to be bought and Sandman did the buying.'

'With money obtained by Roper?'

'That's right.'

'Vintner wasn't a director, though.'

'Don't be silly! I beg your pardon. Excuse me. I didn't mean that. But on no account had Vintner to appear connected with the land companies. He'd have gone to gaol for corrupt practices if that had come out. His control had to be exercised through a nominee on the boards. John Willie Dodd, his son-in-law. He wasn't his son-in-law at that time, though. Vintner had come across him in connection with business at Excelsior and took a fancy to him. He was impressed by what he thought was his ability and prudence. He wasn't much of a judge of character, was he? Dodd was just a big bag of bluff, but he deceived the alderman. By gad, he did! I don't suppose at first he knew what he was getting into. He thought it was just an investment the alderman hadn't time to take care of himself. But I'll bet he soon guessed.'

'And he married the alderman's daughter.'

'He had to. He'd put her in the family way. Vintner's trusted henchman had a roving eye. Her brothers forced the issue and he had to marry her. I can imagine the alderman's feelings when he heard of it. Dodd as his son-in-law! It couldn't have turned out worse. But that wasn't the end of the matter. Sandman died.'

'Suddenly?'

'No. He was ill a long time, gradually growing worse. Dying on his feet. If he'd died and left his Pook's Retreat and the other shares for probate, the whole affair might have come out and incriminated Vintner and others. When he knew there was no hope for him, Sandman arranged for all his interests in land to be transferred to his wife and daughter. They sailed very close to the wind with that probate, but they got a good solicitor and the shares of the various trusts went through at next to nothing. The land was taken at the price paid for it, less the mortgages Roper had financed it with, which cancelled out the value. You see, the new town hadn't started then and land prices hadn't risen much.'

'The lawyer?'

'That's what brought Mr. Ash in the picture.'

'I thought so. And you knowing all this, they paid you a mere hundred a year to keep it confidential, Mr. Bugler?'

'They made me a present now and again... I put that away for a rainy day.'

That was another story. Bugler might have proved another Uriah Heep, spinning his web, if he hadn't had desperate men like Vintner to deal with. As it was, he might have been indulging in a pretty piece of blackmail. However...

'And what was Dodd up to when he met his death?'

Bugler raised a hand as though to fend off evil luck.

'Don't ask me. All I did was act as secretary. The rest, what I've told you, I picked up here and there from minutes and such like.'

'Dodd and his wife, Vintner's daughter, quarrelled?'

'They both quarrelled with Vintner first.'

'That must have been embarrassing for Vintner.'

'He had Dodd nailed by a general deed of trust, for what it was worth. The alderman must have found out the true Dodd as time went on. Then, when Dodd started after other women, his wife and he quarrelled. She didn't go back to her father, however. I don't know why. She's just come back to him now, they tell me. I suppose with Dodd out of the way, it's easier for them.'

'Do you think Alderman Vintner murdered Dodd?'

'That's for you to find out. I know nothing about it. It might have been anybody. And why murder two other innocent parties? Fallows and Piper never did Vintner any harm.'

Bugler sat quietly at his desk, fingering papers and eyeing his calculating machine, as though somehow he derived comfort from the familiar things of his new job. The way in which he had so quickly settled down with Scriboma gave Littlejohn an idea.

'You've been betting for a long time?'

'Who told you...?'

And that explained many things.

Littlejohn lit his pipe and rose to go.

'There's only one other matter I think you ought to attend to, Mr. Bugler. Call a directors' meeting of the Pook's Retreat Development Company and other trusts right away...'

'But I can't do that off my own bat. I've never done such a thing before.'

'Who, then, has called the directors together in the past?'

'Mr. Hartley Ash...'

'Alderman Vintner's lawyer?'

'Yes. Why are you doing this?'

'I want to discuss several matters with them.'

'You won't need me there...'

'As secretary, isn't it part of your duties?'

'It needn't be. Once or twice when I've been ill or away, Mr. Ash has acted for me. If I'm called with the rest and you start questioning them the way you've done me, they'll smell a rat right away and say I've been talking. I couldn't face it.'

'Very well. I'll speak to Mr. Ash and if I think after that that you ought to be there, I'll let you know.'

'Do your best to keep me out of it. I've co-operated with you. In fact, I've talked far more than I should have done and it won't do me any good.'

'Did Alderman Vintner attend any of the meetings?'

'Of course not. Haven't I told you that he never came within a mile of the meetings. His part of the whole business was latterly done through Mr. Roper.'

'Where is Ash's office?'

'Next door to the town hall. You can't miss it. There's a new block of offices.'

'Right. See you later.'

'Not at the meeting. Don't forget.'

Littlejohn went out the way he'd come in; by the dark corridor and down the stairs. There was a strong smell of Mr. Scriboma's cigar in the vicinity, but he himself was nowhere about.

Mr. Ash was in his office, the windows of which overlooked the rates department of the town hall in which people were scuttering around like ants.

The office itself was a bit flashy, like its owner. The carpet was too red and too deep for a place of business and the desk and chairs, copies of antiques, gave the place a phoney opulence. Mr. Ash was apparently a fond parent, too. Here and there were photographs of groups of children, obviously his many offspring, for without exception, all five of them strongly resembled him.

The lawyer was smoking a cigar. It smelled inferior to that of Mr. Scriboma, but Mr. Ash seemed to be greatly enjoying it.

'To what do we owe this pleasure, Superintendent?'

'May I sit down?'

'Of course, if you're going to be here for long. Cigar? Drink then? No? I suppose you're on duty.'

Mr. Ash was altogether too smooth. The kind of lawyer who might mix himself up in income tax or death duties evasion, or finally bolt with his clients' funds.

'I understand you're on the board of the Pook's Retreat Development Company, sir.'

Mr. Ash's cigar slid from his lips to the floor. He rescued it before it could set fire to the carpet, wiped it on his handkerchief, and thrust it between his teeth again. Then he puffed strenuously to revive it, like someone administering the kiss of life to an almost expired victim. He ended up successfully in a fog of smoke.

'Pook's Retreat. Surely the police aren't interested in that. It's a private development company of which I'm the solicitor.'

He had recovered his aplomb.

'An investment trust remotely engaged in buying up local building sites and selling them at substantial profits.'

'Well? Nothing wrong with that, is there? Nothing to do with the police.'

'The murdered man, Dodd, was a director.'

'Sorry to lose him. But where do we go from there?'

'He was the son-in-law of Alderman Vintner, who knows before it's made public which plots in the town are likely to interest the corporation or other eager buyers.'

Mr. Ash, for something better to do, tapped the ash from his cigar into an overflowing ash-tray and rose and closed the window, as though about to suffocate Littlejohn in a fug of smoke.

'Be careful, Superintendent. You may be called upon to substantiate that statement. It's almost an accusation of shady dealing...'

His back was to Littlejohn as he said it.

'I don't think that would be very difficult, Mr. Ash.'

The lawyer spun round, as though about to attack Littlejohn, changed his mind, and sat again at his desk. He looked ready to settle the problem by asking 'How much?'

'But I didn't call for that, Mr. Ash. I've been asking Bugler, secretary of the Pook's Retreat group, to call a directors' meeting. He tells me, however, that you are the convenor.'

'Why a directors' meeting? You're investigating the explosion at Excelsior works, aren't you? What has that to do with Pook's Retreat? And in any case, if I did call the directors to a meeting, you couldn't attend. You've no standing.'

'Yes, I could attend. This time. If it isn't done my way, it will be done much more unpleasantly and with a maximum of publicity through other channels.'

'Such as…?'

'You mentioned shady dealing just now, sir. More politely that is called corrupt practices. There are ways which you, as a lawyer, will know very well, of dealing with those kind of transactions in public affairs.'

'What are you driving at, Littlejohn? What good would a directors' meeting do in this case?'

'It's simply a matter of your co-operation, Mr. Ash. If you call them together here, in your office, it will save our having to invite them to the police station, which might lead to some unhappy publicity. You can explain, if you like, that the death of Mr. Roper has raised certain problems which must be dealt with at once. Get them here, sir. Also, arrange for Alderman Vintner to be here, as well.'

'But that will be impossible! Vintner isn't a director. He'd…'

'He'd smell a rat?'

'What do you mean by that?'

'The success of the trusts depends upon the information which the alderman has given in the past. If he doesn't hold shares, I'm sure he has loan monies, which yield very substantial sums in interest in the companies.'

Ash was ready to come down on the side of the law. No more evasion. He knew what was best for him.

'As a solicitor, I'm bound to support the law, but the alderman won't attend here if he knows there's a directors' meeting of the Pook's Retreat group going on at the time I ask him to call. He daren't...'

'Try him.'

'But the directors are all friends of his. One or the other of them will tell him about the meeting as soon as they receive notice.'

'I'll risk that.'

'Well, don't blame me. I'll do as you ask. Do I invite Bugler as well?'

'Yes.'

Ash fidgeted about a bit and ended by lighting another cigar, this time without much enthusiasm.

'By the way, you understand that I'm simply on the board as their solicitor. I'm not there in an executive capacity; merely advisory.'

'Advisory? In what way?'

'I do the conveyancing of the properties in which the trusts invest.'

'But you surely have had some idea of what has been going on. The women on the board were guinea-pig directors, weren't they?'

'Dodd and Roper saw the deals through. They were the ones who received information and reports on suitable properties for investment.'

'From Vintner?'

'I don't know. As I said before, you'd better be careful before you accuse Vintner of corruption. Very careful.'

Ash was recovering his confidence somewhat.

'I can assure you of that.'

'You are aware, by the way, that with the deaths of Dodd and Roper, there are now only three directors of the trusts: myself and Mrs. Sandman and her daughter, Mrs. Hoop?'

'Yes.'

'Why call a meeting, then?'

'I'd prefer it that way, if you please. And don't forget to include the arrangement for Alderman Vintner to be in the other room. We might wish to call him into the meeting.'

Mr. Ash looked blankly at the window as though contemplating jumping through it.

'I'd advise you not to antagonise the alderman, Superintendent. He's a very formidable adversary, I can assure you.'

'So I gather. You, I assume, will take the chair at the company meeting, sir. I'm sure you'll be well able to handle him.'

Mr. Ash was on his knees on the carpet seeking again the cigar which had slipped from his open mouth.

CROMWELL HALTED THE POLICE CAR AT THE LARGE NOTICE-board which reared up at the roadside.

ROSEALBA QUARRIES LIMITED WARNING
BLASTING IN OPERATION WHEN THE RED FLAG IS SHOWN

'Pity someone didn't show the red flag for poor old Dodd,' he said to himself.

There was no flag flying, so he went on his way. Soon he came upon the quarries, a huge gash in the landscape between the main Brighton Road and Baron's Sterndale.

There didn't seem to be much going on there. The workings stood on high ground. A few sheds, an office, the quarries themselves and the cumbersome machinery of the trade, some in the open, some under cover of roughly constructed buildings. Over all, a dim November mist which seemed to seep into your bones.

Finally Cromwell found the workmen gathered in a group. About eight or nine of them, under cover, squatting or sitting on old boxes or anything else available. It was lunch time and they were warming themselves at a coke brazier. All around them were spread the quarried blocks of stone, some of them roughly dressed; others in the raw, with heaps of chippings scattered about.

The men around the fire took little interest in Cromwell at first. They mistook him for a busybody, passing by and briefly nosing into what was going on. He was treated as an intruder.

But Cromwell was not the type you could ignore for long. His ready smile and modest integrity seemed to appeal to one of the men at least. He rose and went to meet the Inspector.

'Looking for somebody?'

'The manager or the foreman.'

'I'm the foreman.'

A medium built, middle-aged countryman, with an intelligent face and an appearance of immense physical strength. It was obvious he was puzzled about Cromwell, trying hard to size him up.

'I'm from the police and I'd be glad if you could spare me a minute or two, if I'm not disturbing your lunch.'

'I've finished…'

To prove it, he took out a short pipe and a metal tobacco box, from which he cut a piece of plug which he started to rub between the palms of his hands. He nodded in the direction of the shed labelled *Office*.

'Let's go in there. It's warmer.'

They scrambled their way across the blocks of stone followed by the now inquisitive looks of the rest of the workmen.

A plain wooden shanty with a few bare chairs about, a desk, a table covered with papers, an old safe, a very old clock on the wall stopped at 4.45 and a time-punching machine for the workmen with another clock embodied in it. This one registered 12.45, which reminded Cromwell that he hadn't eaten since breakfast. The whole place was dusty.

'Sit down.'

The man wiped two chairs with a duster which he produced from a drawer and threw his cap on the desk. Then he switched on an old electric fire, which took an unconscionable time to show any signs of life.

'What can I do for you? It isn't often we have a visit from the police. Is it poachers or another banknote snatch?'

He spoke with the pleasant intonation of the locality.

'No. It's about the explosion at the Excelsior office in Evingden.'

'Oh, that. The bank raid and the little girl being stabbed have put Evingden out of the headlines, haven't they? What has the explosion to do with Rosealba quarries?'

'We're trying to find out where the dynamite came from.'

'We've plenty here and we had some pinched during the summer. But I don't expect it was used in Evingden. We got the idea that either some teddy-boys had been at it out of sheer mischief, or else some of the London gangs had whipped it for one of their jobs.'

'Do you use much blasting powder here?'

'Not very much. This is a freestone quarry where the stuff is easy to work. We quarry it in large blocks for building and smaller ones for other sorts of jobs and it yields easily to machinery. Now and then, we have to blast when we start a fresh run...'

'You keep a good supply of what is it...? Dynamite? Gelignite?'

'Dynamite. We're old-fashioned. Besides, years ago, one of our directors bought a large stock of it, cheaply, he thought, but far too much.'

'Our experts tell us that the old sort of dynamite was used for the Excelsior job, so it's quite on the cards the stuff stolen from you was employed.'

'Was it, by hell! So it *was* pinched by teddy-boys, was it?'

'We don't know. That's why I'm here. When was your stock broken into?'

'Last August. I know that because I was away on holidays at the time. It wasn't broken into. It was just nicked... picked-up, as you might say. The stock's kept in boxes of a dozen and one of them was open, with four sticks left. That was all that went. I said at the time one of our own men had taken it. Useful in poaching fish, you know. Dynamiting a pond or river. The blast kills the fish, they float to the surface and you scoop 'em out. I was mad about it. It's a dangerous game having loose dynamite lying around. I questioned the men. Some of them would be quite up to such tricks and when I didn't get any further, I sent for the local policeman, who happens to be my son...'

He nodded proudly.

'That's why I'm ready to help you all I can.'

'Thanks, Mr....?'

'Gatton's the name.'

'Mr. Gatton. I don't suppose he was able to get very far with the case, was he? I've had similar ones myself and they've come to nothing.'

'That's right. Short of torturing them or one of them splitting on another, there wasn't a hope. We left it at that. Until the Evingden police came enquiring about an explosion at a bank there. Then, we began to think that, some way or other, some of the local bad lads had swiped the dynamite when nobody was lookin', although it's kept in a brick shed with a steel door.'

'I suppose it's left open until the gang leaves work?'

'Very often it is. We keep other odds and ends in the same shed and have to open it from time to time. It might be left unlocked then, till I lock up at night.'

'Had strangers been seen around at the time of the theft?'

'There's always somebody passing. It's quite a well-used by-road, you know. Plenty of cars take the short cut across the hill.'

'So I see. But was anyone seen prowling around the quarry about that time?'

'Not particularly. We have visitors now and then. The directors come up about once a month after their meeting, which is held in Evingden. Our registered office is there. They make a point of inspecting the quarry and the stock, you know.'

'Who are the directors?'

'It's a family affair. In the old days, it belonged to the Pochins. Then, the family died out. All girls, who got married and then the husbands of two of them looked after the business. Mr. Sandman, who married a Miss Beatrice Pochin, took over after the death of his wife's brother, Mr. Rupert. Now there was a businessman for you. Mr. Sandman. This firm was getting on its last legs when Mr. Rupert caved in. Drink did it. Mr. Sandman put the whole show on its feet again. Pity he died so soon. Mr. Flaxley's chairman now. He married another Miss Pochin.'

'Is Mr. Sandman's widow still interested in the concern?'

'Sure. She's on the board. She was the best of the Pochins. She was always interested in the quarries. Used to come riding up here on a lively horse before she married. A cut above Sandman she was, but there's no accounting for taste.'

'Was there a directors' meeting here about the time the dynamite vanished?'

'Yes. They came as usual after the monthly meeting. Why? Thinking one of them might have helped himself to some blasting sticks?'

'Just routine, that's all. What would they want with dynamite?'

'You're right. Miss Beatrice was the only one who understood anything about it. The rest are just businessmen. Miss Beatrice… Mrs. Sandman, that is… could have handled it. She knew everything that went on in quarrying in her day. She was up here so much, you see. It was a pleasant ride on her horse from Brantwood, where they lived, up to Rosealba. She used to stay here and drink tea with the men and enquire all about the jobs. Not much about freestone she didn't know, either.'

'Where do you buy your explosives?'

'As I said, Mr. Rupert bought a big stock. I fancy a London traveller must have got at him when he'd had one over the eight, and sold it to him.'

'I wondered if there was somewhere in Evingden that would sell it.'

'No. Who could there be in a place like Evingden? And who would want to buy it?'

'I saw a big ironmonger's there. Viner's... Vinters... What was the name?'

'Vintner's. No fear. It's owned by a big-head called Alderman Vintner. He's very lame. Know how? Explosives. He used to sell guns and cartridges. One day the shop got on fire right under the stock of sporting cartridges. The lot went up, with the alderman on top of 'em. Nearly killed him. He lost his leg up to the knee. After that, he wouldn't have a gun or a cartridge about the place. Scared. The shock must have given him a sort of mental kink against them. Catch him with dynamite anywhere near him. Not likely.'

'Where do your firm bank?'

The man looked surprised.

'Funny question in an explosion enquiry, isn't it?'

'As I said before, mere routine, you know.'

'It won't be telling secrets to say that we bank in Evingden. Poor old Roper, who drowned himself at Brighton, was our manager. I wonder what made him do it. Perhaps he was wrong in his books, or a brain storm, or something. You never know when it will come, do you? It might be you or me tomorrow.'

Cromwell nodded sympathetically.

'Did Roper ever come here?'

'You think he pinched the dynamite and then drowned himself because he heard the police were enquiring about it? What would he do with dynamite? Blast open his safes instead of using a key?'

'Routine!'

'You and your routine! You're deeper than you try to make out, Inspector. Well, take a load of this. Mr. Roper did come up with the directors in August. He came every quarter. You see, there's a bank loan against the quarries and the manager calls regularly to see that nobody's run away with them.'

Cromwell's heart sank and his face lengthened. He'd expected to narrow down matters to one suspect. Now, he was being showered, overwhelmed with them. In a despairing gesture of masochism he asked, almost shouted: 'Do you know Oswald Bugler? Does he ever come up here?'

Gatton gave Cromwell a sly look. He was wondering whether or not to admit it.

'I might as well tell you now, that what he was doing isn't illegal any more. He came nearly every week in his old car. He was a bookie's runner for his brother-in-law, Bert Scriboma. He collected bets and football pool monies from the men here.'

In fact, the quarry seemed to have been a public thoroughfare for all the suspects in the case!

Cromwell went on with the torture.

'What about Alderman Vintner?'

'Never. Did you see that notice about blasting? The very sight of it would make the alderman run a mile the other way. I told you, didn't I, about his accident?'

'That's right. Do you know Fred Hoop?'

'Only by name. Read about his financial misfortune in the papers. The only director of Excelsior joinery in Evingden that hasn't been wiped out. What a state to be in. Wondering when it's going to be your turn. If you're thinking about whether he visited the quarry, the answer's no, he didn't. What's all this about, in any case? Is it the dynamite? Because if it is, I think you're barking up the wrong tree.'

'Would it be possible for you to ask your workmen about any of them being around the dynamite store and behaving suspiciously in August, at the time when the sticks were missed?'

'It's a long time ago. Still, I don't mind asking. As I said, my son's in the force and I'm always ready to oblige a policeman. I'll ask. All our men were here in August. We don't often change hands in our business. Coming?'

They toured the hard, rough ground of the quarry and the stony workings wherever a man was busy. Did any of the visitors in August show particular interest in blasting operations or the dynamite and where it was stored? No; they didn't. The answer came from first one man, then another. The question brought forth sarcastic remarks about the length of time and the tax on a man's memory. Until, finally, patience was rewarded.

A small, wiry man in a big cap and a duffle coat which had seen better days thought he remembered something. It might have been in August, or even early September. August, because the football season hadn't started and the Scriboma pools weren't running.

'That little chap, Trumpeter...'

'Bugler?'

'Bugler. That's him. I recollect him suddenly gettin' interested in blasting here. Said he'd not noticed the warning notice till then. Well, one thing led to another and he said he'd never seen a stick of dynamite. I told him if he'd give me a good tip for the 3.30 next day, I'd show him one. He did, too, and it won me a couple of quid.'

'What happened?'

'Took him to the explosive shed, which wasn't locked on account of our checking stock for the directors arrivin'. I showed him a stick of dynamite and he said now he'd know.'

'Was that all?'

'Yes. Should there be more?'

'Did you leave him alone in the shed or near it?'

The man spat out his diminutive cigarette end and slowly raised his huge cap from his brows as though to facilitate deep thinking.

'Let me think. Yes. While we were in the shed, he said thanks for showing him and he gave me the tip for next day then and there. I owed him half-a-crown for my last bet and when I offered him a ten-bob note, he said he'd no change and could I ask one of the chaps if they could change the note. Which struck me as funny as he'd been collecting money all over the place. I hadn't any change myself, so I crossed to Fred Kinnan and got it from him.'

'Leaving Bugler in the explosive store?'

'No. I took him outside and asked him to wait there, after I'd closed the door. I wasn't running any risks.'

'Did you lock the door?'

'No. I was only away a couple of minutes.'

'He'd time to go back and take another look if he wished?'

'Yes, I suppose he had, but why should he want to? He'd seen all he wanted, hadn't he?'

Cromwell thanked the man in the cap, shook Gatton's hand heartily and thanked him, too. He also said he wished Gatton's son, who was in the force, the best of luck.

Then he almost ran back to his car. In his haste, he passed through a built-up area exceeding the speed limit, and was stopped by P.C. Gatton, who solemnly took out his notebook. Cromwell equally solemnly took out his warrant-card, and all was well.

DYNAMITE DISAPPEARS

'WHAT DID YOU DO WITH THE DYNAMITE YOU TOOK FROM the Rosealba quarries?'

'Oh, God!!'

That was all Bugler could say at first. He broke into a sweat which brought drops like peas across his bald front, turned the colour of putty, and then sprawled across the desk with his head in his hands.

Littlejohn had sent Cromwell to bring him to the police station. Not an arrest, Bugler was told, but the need for more help in the case. Remembering the aroma of cigar smoke which had accompanied their last interview, he was giving Scriboma no more chances of eavesdropping behind the door.

Bugler had arrived looking apprehensive. He'd had something on his mind throughout the investigation and now he was faced with it.

'So, it's as bad as that, is it, Mr. Bugler? What made you wish to blow up the offices and kill three men into the bargain?'

Bugler leapt to his feet like someone stung.

'I never... I'd nothing to do with the Excelsior explosion...'

'But you took the dynamite. Why?'

Bugler was too confused to deny it. He was too busy struggling to disentangle himself from the Green Lane murders.

'I never even used it.'

'Why did you take it then?'

'I never even used it.'

'You'd better tell me who did. Otherwise, we shall assume that you were responsible for the Excelsior disaster. Let's begin at the beginning.'

It took Bugler a long time to make up his mind which way to speak. He seemed torn between alternatives, but obviously decided that murder was the greater.

'My brother-in-law asked me to get it for him.'

'Scriboma. Why? What did he want with dynamite? You'd better make a clean breast of it, Mr. Bugler. There's no easy way out, either for you or Scriboma. Did you marry Scriboma's sister, by the way?'

'I did not. He married my sister. I only had anything to do with him to protect her. I'm all she's got except him. Not that he's not good to her. She *would* marry him and this is where it's landed her. His father came from Turkey or somewhere in that region. A gaolbird for a husband and another for a brother. What a mess!'

'You've soon passed sentence on both of you, haven't you? What have you both been doing? Shall I tell you?'

'If you know, why ask me?'

'Scriboma had taken an office in Elizabeth Street in which to open up his betting shop when it was ready. Two doors away was a new bank without a strong room, using safes to hold the cash temporarily. Scriboma must have watched the arrival of the safes and misjudged their strength. He also cased the building from his lookout above the street. He decided to try his luck on the cash safe when convenient. He failed miserably.'

'*He* didn't do it. He couldn't open a sardine tin properly. It was a friend of his from London.'

'Who?'

'I don't know. You'll have to ask Bert Scriboma. All I did was to get the explosive.'

'Why didn't the professional operator bring his own materials?'

'That's what I said. But it seems the police had their eye on him for another job and to be found buying or in possession of "jelly" or anything like it would probably be the finish of him. Bert said he'd get the stuff himself,'

'So, he told *you* to get it. Why you?'

'He knew I went to the quarries regularly on business...'

'Scriboma's business?'

'Yes. Collecting and paying out to the men.'

'But how did he manage to persuade you to steal the dynamite? You know that's what it was, don't you?'

'Yes.'

'Well?'

'I got into financial trouble and Bert helped me out.'

'Helped you out of what?'

A pause, whilst Bugler put the pros and cons to himself again.

'A forged cheque.'

'On whose account?'

'Excelsior...'

Bugler sat upright and thumped the table in rage.

'I was never paid properly or promptly. So, I drew a cheque myself...'

'How much?'

'Two hundred. It wasn't much for all I'd done.'

'You looked after Excelsior books and hoped to fiddle it through?'

'You can put it that way, if you like.'

'You forged the signature?'

'Two of them. Yes. Fred Hoop's and Dodd's.'

'How did Scriboma come into this?'

'The cheque bounced. Dodd got a cheque in before me and Roper dishonoured the one I'd forged. Not because of the signatures, which passed muster, but for lack of funds in the Excelsior account! I've never had any luck.'

'Well?'

'I'd made it payable to myself as though it might have been for arrears of wages. I thought I could handle it better that way. Besides we always made cheques for wages and petty cash out to me. I paid it into my own bank, the City and Counties, and drew a cheque for £150 on them in favour of Scriboma.'

'Betting?'

'Yes.'

'And when the Excelsior cheque bounced from Home Counties, yours to Scriboma also bounced from City and Counties?'

'That's it.'

'Even then...'

'Bert played merry hell and said he ought to see me in gaol for issuing dud cheques.'

'But he didn't.'

'No. He kept my cheque that had bounced and took the one I'd forged, too, and said he was going down to see Dodd about the Excelsior cheque and raise Cain. I couldn't let him do that, could I? I had to tell him what I'd done. He actually laughed, put both cheques in his safe, and said sometime after I'd done him a good turn, he'd tear them both up.'

'And the good turn was the dynamite.'

'That's what it amounted to. Is that all? Scriboma'll wonder what I'm doing out so long.'

'It looks very much as if he won't be bothering much longer about where you or anybody else is. No; I've still one or two more questions. As a matter of interest, what happened at the bank?'

'Scriboma's friend couldn't have been a professional, after all. Just a silly muddler. I don't know exactly what happened. I'm no expert. All I know is they roused the town early in the morning, brought down the ceiling of the bank and blew out the windows, but didn't make any impression on the safe at all. All my trouble for nothing.'

'How much dynamite did they use?'

'I gave four sticks to Bert. He'd said to get two sticks, but I was pushed at the quarries and didn't know what I was doing when I took four. There was no time, you see. I was just able to grab what I could.'

'They didn't use four?'

'No. They only used two. Bert hung on to the other two. Then on the day before the Excelsior fire, Bert gave the two back to me. "Get rid of those quick," he said. His friend, Spicer, the one who tried to open the safe, had been picked up by the police. Bert thought that if Spicer spilled the beans about the Evingden bank break-in and the police decided to give Bert's place the once-over, it would be a bit awkward if they found the dynamite there.'

'So, Scriboma passed the hot potatoes to you? What did you do with them?'

'I didn't know how to dispose of them. I couldn't very well take them back to the quarries, could I? And it wouldn't have been right to put them in the dustbin or on a rubbish tip. Kids might have got them and done harm to themselves.'

'You did have scruples then?'

'Of course I did. It's different a crook blasting open a safe from kids killing or maiming themselves. I finally took the two sticks and hid them in my filing cabinet at the Excelsior. I thought they'd be all right there. I had in mind taking them and throwing them in a river, or else in the sea as soon as I'd the time.'

'But you didn't.'

'No. Before I could do it, somebody took them.'

'Why didn't you tell us all this after the explosion? It would have saved us a lot of time and trouble.'

'Tell you the dynamite *I'd* pinched had been pinched from me! That would have been very clever of me, wouldn't it? You'd have said I'd invented the whole story and accused me of blowing up Dodd and the others myself.'

'Who took the dynamite from your office? Any idea?'

'I don't know. The cabinet was locked most of the time. I kept the key.'

'How many keys were there?'

'I had one, and Dodd and Fred Hoop had the other two, in case I was away. I was the only one who used the cabinet, though.'

'Was it under your eye all day until you left at night?'

'Yes.'

'With the sticks of dynamite loose in it?'

'No. I put them in a cardboard box that had once had screws in it.'

'What kind of box?'

'Just large enough to hold three or four sticks. It was one of Forest and Hedley's old boxes.'

'How long were the sticks of dynamite there?'

'Just that day. Scriboma met me with them on my way to work. I couldn't get rid of them right away and that night I couldn't either. I'd something on. So I left them locked in the office cabinet.'

At this point, Cromwell put in his head. Littlejohn and Bugler had been at it so long that he had begun to wonder if anything had gone wrong. The sight of Littlejohn's slow-burning pipe and Bugler's flushed features reassured him.

'All right?'

'Yes. We won't be long now.'

In the town outside, the opening blows of a parliamentary by-election were being struck. A parading loudspeaker van was praising one of the candidates. 'Let's have a change this time. Vote for Moody.'

'And the two sticks of dynamite were stolen.'

'That's right. They vanished.'

'Did anyone use the cabinet besides you?'

'Not usually. It had the men's time-sheets in it.'

'Did you see anybody looking in the drawer? Or did you leave anyone alone in your office whilst the dynamite was there?'

Bugler thought for a minute.

'Anybody might have wandered in and if I wasn't there, they could have pried in the drawers and perhaps seen it. I was always in and out of the drawers, but on that day, I locked it as often as I remembered. I hadn't been in the habit of locking it till then, except when I left at night. Remembering to lock it every time I used it while the dynamite was there needed a bit of getting into. I did forget a time or two, but when I recollected what was in it, I quickly shut and locked it.'

'Did you see Fred Hoop around?'

'No.'

'Anyone at all?'

'Old Tom Hoop came in about the time-sheets. He took them away but he didn't find the dynamite. I remember checking that it hadn't been interfered with after he left. I must admit that when he calmly opened the drawer and said he wanted the sheets, it gave me a bit of a turn. I held my breath till he'd taken them.'

'He came later and replaced them?'

'Not exactly. He put them on my desk when he'd finished with them. I was out of the room at the time and had locked the cabinet when I left.'

'Any other callers? You seem to be able to remember quite a lot when you make an effort.'

'I'm not holding back deliberately. After all that's happened lately, it's a wonder I can remember anything. Other callers, did you say? Yes. Alderman Vintner called about a bill we'd owed him for more than six months. He was in a terrible temper and said he was going to issue a writ right away if we didn't pay up at once. He used to allow the company long credit till he quarrelled with Dodd.'

'What about?'

'You ought to know. It's all over the town. The way Dodd treated Alderman Vintner's daughter, his wife. Having affairs with other women. The alderman fancies himself a big shot in Evingden and naturally objected to having his family name dragged in the mud.'

'You say he called…'

'Yes. I said he'd better talk to Dodd. He said he'd been in the main office already, but found Dodd telephoning. He told me to tell Dodd that he was going to his lawyer right away. He worked himself up into such a rage that I thought he'd have a stroke on the spot. He seemed to blame me as well as Dodd.'

'Why?'

'He was out for blood. "I hear Forest and Hedley are sup- plying you with ironmongery now. Do they know the financial state you're in? I'll soon let them know. I'll stop your credit with them and everybody else." That's what he said to me, as if I'd done it all.'

'How did he know about Forest and Hedley?'

'I don't know. Perhaps they'd told him. They were very good to us after Vintner cut us off. They supplied us with hinges, screws, nails and the like.'

'Did Vintner have a chance to see the dynamite?'

'I don't think so. I was there all the time the alderman was in the office. I might have turned my back for a minute while I got out the overdue bills from a drawer behind my desk. I don't remember.'

'Was that the same morning that Tom Hoop came for the time-sheets?'

'Yes, it was. About half an hour before Vintner arrived.'

'Did you check that the dynamite was still there when you locked up at night?'

'I'd locked the cabinet when I went to lunch and I didn't open it again. I was sure the dynamite hadn't been interfered with. You see, Fleming, the shop steward, called just as I was putting my things away. It was half-past five and he said he wanted to see me. It was about wages for the week, as usual. I said wouldn't it do in the morning, as I was in a hurry. He said if I'd lock up, he'd walk home with me and tell me what he wanted then. I couldn't shake him off. I didn't open the cabinet again. In any case I couldn't have looked to see if the dynamite was still there. Fleming was breathing down my neck. So, as I was sure it hadn't been tampered with, I left without checking it.'

'When did Tom Hoop first stay away with his last illness?'

'He was taken unwell soon after he came for the time-sheets. They persuaded him to go home. He was very ill later that day and at night they said he was very bad. I think it must have been his heart.'

'When did you actually find the dynamite missing?'

'It must have been taken on the day I put it there, the day of the explosion. I can't imagine who or how. As I told you, I was there all the time. Once or twice, I half hesitated about taking it away with me the same night and getting rid of it right away, but I'd to play in a snooker match at half-past eight. So I decided to leave it another day.'

'You first discovered its disappearance the morning after the fire?'

'Before that. I went to my office to get hold of it and put it somewhere safely out of the way while the fire was burning. I thought if the flames or even the heat spread across the street to the main buildings, and reached my office, there'd be another explosion and the whole of the works would go up.'

'The dynamite in your drawer was obviously taken and used to blow up the main offices.'

'That's what it looks like. You'd better not think I did it, because I didn't.'

'Where were you when the explosion occurred?'

'I was waiting for that. Well, I've got a cast-iron alibi. I was in the Queen's Arms in the centre of Evingden from seven till just after eight, when the news came that Excelsior works were on fire. It was the night of our snooker handicap, due to begin at eight. It didn't, because of the fire. I was in the Arms early to have a drink and a chat with the rest. The landlord and a dozen or more others will tell you I was with them all the time.'

'Very well, Mr. Bugler. Just one last enquiry. About what time did Tom Hoop call for the time-sheets?'

'Half-past ten. I was just having my morning cup of tea.'

'And Vintner?'

'Oh, about eleven.'

'Anyone else call?'

'You asked that before. I was out a lot of the time in the works. I locked the cabinet every time I left my office.'

'Right. Please don't leave town until this matter has been squared up. You're an important witness and I might need you again.'

'What's going to happen about me for taking the dynamite from the quarry?'

'We'll talk about that later. I won't forget the straightforward way you've helped me.'

Bugler was still uneasy.

'Scriboma will kill me when he gets to know what I've told you. You forced me to say some very unpleasant things about Bert.'

'I forced you to do nothing. I didn't even caution you. You simply decided to co-operate with the police because that's the right thing to do. Leave it at that. It will serve you in good stead. Meanwhile, not a word to Scriboma about this interview or what you've said about his part in the bank attempt.'

'He knows I'm here. He's sure to ask.'

'Simply tell him, then, we've been questioning you closely about the finances and other business of Excelsior. That's all.'

Bugler left with melodramatic gestures of caution and care, as though his brother-in-law might have been listening behind the door and waiting for a chance to despatch him without more ado.

Littlejohn was glad to see the last of Bugler. He'd received a report from Cromwell about the surfeit of suspects which he'd accumulated at the Rosealba quarries. Now, Littlejohn was getting his share. He needed time to think. He also needed a bit of peace and quiet, for the loudmouth amplifier was under the windows again.

'We need a change. Vote for Moody this time.'

14

DIRECTORS' MEETING

THERE WAS STILL A POLICEMAN ON DUTY AT THE WRECK
of the Excelsior offices, to keep away the species of beach-
combers who kept hanging round in the hope of salvaging something valuable from the ruins. The bobby saluted Littlejohn
smartly.

'Is Mr. Fred Hoop about? They told me I'd probably find him
here.'

'He's never away, sir. You'll find him in the works. He's established his headquarters in the works office. I don't know what he's
doing all the time. Perhaps trying to rebuild the company.'

Fred Hoop was there, in Bugler's office. He looked up at
Littlejohn blankly from a pile of ledgers he was scrutinising.

There were books and papers piled high on the desk, on tables
and on the floor. Some of them were charred; others were so old
that they might have dated back to the foundation of the firm in
happier days, and looked ready to fall to bits.

'Can't you see I'm busy?'

He was like one of those persistent insects, pursuing an inter-
minable instinctive course which leads nowhere. His pale hatchet
face protruded over a pile of scorched papers from which he
seemed to have created a stack of notes. His eyes glowed feverishly
in their sunken orbits and he hadn't had a shave, which made his
cheeks more grimy and hollower. He looked as if he'd recently
been sleeping in his clothes as well.

'I won't keep you long, Mr. Hoop.'

'If it's anything about the explosion case, I've nothing more to say. I'm now busy trying to make the best of a bad job. It's awful. I don't know where to begin.'

He looked it, too!

He waved a grubby hand at Littlejohn.

'As for the murder case, if such it was, it looks as if that's a washout, too. You police keep messing about and doing nothing. It'll probably end up unsolved.'

'We're still trying, at least.'

The same could be said for Fred Hoop, judging from the piles of work he was attempting to fathom.

'I want to ask you one or two more questions.'

Fred Hoop extricated himself from the mass of rubbish surrounding him and faced Littlejohn across the wreckage on the desk. He looked to have lost a lot of weight, too, in the few days since the disaster.

'I ought to have my lawyer with me. I intended doing that all the time. But now I don't care. I don't care if you arrest me. I'm fed up with it all. Ask your questions. I don't care. I shan't answer them if I don't want.'

A little more and he'd burst into tears of despair.

'Sit down, sir. I'm only asking for help and you won't incriminate yourself at all by answering. First of all, though, your account of what you did on the night of the fire isn't quite straight.'

'Do you think I made it all up? You can check it, can't you? It's a pity you haven't something better to do…'

'You stated that you left your father's house about seven. You then went home and had some tea, later leaving for Brantwood, where your wife was staying with her mother. You arrived there at eight.'

'Well? All that's true. As I said…'

'Your wife said you arrived at half-past seven.'

'She was wrong. She never was one for caring about the truth. She wouldn't care if her statements hanged me…'

Suddenly Hoop burst out in rage, panting and shaking with it.

'I said eight and it *was* eight!'

He thumped a pile of records, which slid from the table and scattered all over the place.

'You also said you'd called at Brantwood to bring her home. You knew she was staying there and had no intention of returning home.'

It seemed to puncture Hoop's frenzy and he went limp again.

'You seem to know.'

'Let's say, to put the record straight, you called to ask her for money for Excelsior wages and that you appealed to her to come home.'

'If that's the way you want it. It makes no difference to me. I couldn't care less.'

'You told the police you left Mrs. Sandman's house about nine o'clock, but you didn't arrive at Excelsior works until after eleven. Where had you been?'

'I had to change a wheel of my car on the way. A flat tyre. In pouring rain. That's the one and only reason I was so late.'

'Very well. One more question. First, let me say how sorry I was to hear of your father's death…'

Hoop looked all round the room as though seeking something before he finally looked in Littlejohn's direction again. Then, he seemed about to thank him, but changed his mind.

'Well? That won't bring him back. Now I'm left without anybody to help me restore all this mess. The only one left of the whole board of directors.'

'Tell me, Mr. Hoop, on the morning before the fire, did you meet your father in the works with the time-sheets?'

Hoop looked blankly at Littlejohn.

'What about it?'

'Was he unwell then?'

'Yes. I said he'd better go home and take a rest. He'd a pain in his chest. Said it was a cold, but I thought it was his heart. The post-mortem proved I was right. It *was* his heart. There was nothing the matter with his lungs.'

So much for Tom Hoop's medical herbalism!

'He asked you to return the time-sheets to Bugler's office?'

'Yes.'

'Did he make any other remark before he left you to go home?'

'Nothing of any consequence.'

'What do you mean by any consequence, sir?'

'What I say. My father was very unwell at the time and made a rambling comment or two which made me think he was growing a bit delirious.'

Hoop gazed wearily around at the confusion of books and papers surrounding him. Then he passed his hand over his ruffled hair.

'Is that all? I want to get on. Bugler's deserted the ship and the directors are all dead except me. There's nobody left...'

'Did your father mention dynamite before he left you, Mr. Hoop?'

'Yes, he did. He said, "What's Bugler doing with sticks of dynamite in his filing cabinet? Just look into it." And with that he went home, adding that if he hadn't felt so ill, he'd have looked into it himself.'

'Did you do as your father asked?'

'Of course. I thought he didn't quite know what he was talking about, but that I'd better come here and see. It was in this office. There was nobody here and the filing cabinet over there was locked. I had a key to it, so I unlocked it. There was nothing there even resembling dynamite.'

'Was there anything that might once have contained it? An old box which had once held screws?'

'Nothing. I turned out all the drawers. There was nothing there but some more old time-sheets.'

'And then you locked it up again and left the time-sheets your father gave you and went away?'

'Yes. Bugler was nowhere about, so I couldn't ask him what father had meant. I never gave the incident another thought. With all I've had to worry me since…'

Littlejohn felt sorry for him. A helpless and incompetent man doing his best. He'd paid off all the workmen and was quite alone.

'Did you know anything about an offer of £5,000 made for the freehold of these premises?'

Hoop tried to control his agitation with difficulty.

'Who told you that? I thought it was confidential. Somebody approached Dodd with a tentative offer. He mentioned it the afternoon before he died. I told him to tell them to go to hell. My father was ill and I wasn't going to take the responsibility of agreeing to it. In any case, after all the work I'd put in at the Excelsior, I wasn't in favour of selling out at the first signs of adversity.'

By the look of him, he was a bit mad. Recent events had been too much for him. He'd got the whole story of the failure of Excelsior out of perspective and now he was hoping somehow to restore the fortunes of a firm that had never had any good fortune at all. He babbled on now.

'…We've had a lot of worries here and my father's breakdown added to them.'

'I'm very sorry, sir, and I hope you manage to pull things round. Goodbye…'

Hoop was already sorting out his papers again. He bade Littlejohn a vague goodbye without looking up.

Outside, it was raining. A mournful, sickly drizzle which made the wrecked offices and deserted works look more melancholy and hopeless than ever. Littlejohn climbed in the police car. Half an hour later he was in Brantwood, ringing at the doorbell of Pochins again.

At first he thought there was nobody at home; it took them so long to answer. Then Mrs. Sandman appeared. She was smartly dressed and judging from the sound of voices indoors was entertaining a party of women.

'Good afternoon, Superintendent Littlejohn. I'm glad to see you again, although the time's rather inconvenient. I have callers and we're in the midst of tea.'

'Is Mrs. Hoop available?'

'Yes. Shall I ask her to come? If you've anything to say to her, the morning room's available. I won't be a minute.'

She invited him inside and he found himself waiting the way he'd done when he first called there. Judging from the noise of talk they might have been holding a large women's tea-meeting at Pochins.

Mrs. Fred Hoop appeared. She was flushed with excitement and dressed in her best, all her jewellery and all. She greeted Littlejohn almost joyfully. You'd never have thought that her lover had been shockingly killed a few days before. She and Fred Hoop must have been a mad couple. No wonder Tom Hoop had been worried about them.

'Did you wish to see me, Superintendent?'

'Yes, very briefly, Mrs. Hoop. Could we find a place to talk in?'

She led the way to the same small room he'd visited before, leaving a heavy scent of perfume in her wake.

'Now...'

It sounded like a satisfied sigh. She even forgot to offer him a seat.

'On the day of the Excelsior disaster, did John Dodd telephone you? About eleven o'clock. If so, could you tell me what it was about?'

She flushed and even looked coy.

'It was very personal...'

'I understand. But your answer to my question is most important. It will probably help us in finding out who was the murderer.'

She caught her breath. She was slipping into the play-acting rôle again.

'In that case, I must help. But you will see when I tell you, that the matter was very intimate between us. John said he wished to talk with me about... a divorce. You see, don't you, how difficult it is? His wife had been to see a lawyer. He asked if Fred would... well... release *me*, too. I said it was too secret to talk about over the telephone. Actually, I wanted time to think. I hadn't made up my mind about things, you see. John was very excited... So impulsive and emotional... He asked if I could meet him at the office. Excelsior office... at eight o'clock. He'd be alone and we could talk privately. I said yes. Then, he said he'd another piece of news, too. His fortunes looked like being much improved...'

'In what way? Did he tell you?'

'Not in detail. He said he'd do so when we met. He said he'd a big deal on and would soon be in the big money. I asked him to give me a hint of what it was about. It was then his turn to say it was too private to talk about over the telephone. He would give me a hint, though, if I'd keep it secret. It concerned selling the Excelsior business, he said, for a large sum of money.'

'And that was all?'

'For then, yes. But later, in the middle of the afternoon, John rang me up again. He asked me to put off the meeting at the office that evening. He'd a conference about his big deal to attend and would ring me afterwards. He never did, as well you know...'

She poked about in the corners of her eyes with a small lace handkerchief to indicate that she was in tears or well on the way to them, at any rate.

'Thank you, Mrs. Hoop. That's been a great help. I won't take any more of your time.'

She saw him to the door, gave him a theatrical handshake in farewell, and hurried back to her friends. Littlejohn didn't know what she would tell them about the visit, but it was sure to be something fantastic.

After dinner, Littlejohn and Cromwell crossed the town square to the chambers of Mr. Hartley Ash, where the meetings of the various trusts were to be held at half-past seven.

The new town spread around in all its glory, illuminated in pale blue with here and there a dash of flood-lighting to advertise some feature of the place. Large bills announced a couple of political meetings for the imminent by-election, but few people showed any interest. *You Need a Change This Time. Vote for Moody. Vote for Kelly. You Can Trust Him.* Public Choice polls had already moved-in Moody by a large majority and everybody seemed to be leaving it at that.

Lights were burning in Hartley Ash's office. Every room was illuminated as though a civic reception or a cocktail party were expected. When Littlejohn and Cromwell entered there was nobody there except the junior clerk who was reading a comic paper.

'Mr. Ash'll not be a minute.'

The first to arrive after them was Tattersall, who seemed surprised to find nobody else there.

'You did say half-past seven, didn't you?'

He was as breezy as ever.

'I've sent round for Fred Hoop and told him you'd like to see him here about 7.45. The constable who called found him working at the Excelsior books and he didn't seem at all glad of the invitation.'

They were cut short by the arrival of Mr. Ash. His face fell when he saw the three of them.

'I don't know how I'm going to explain the presence of you three at the meeting. It's most irregular.'

'Let me do it, then. I'll take the responsibility.'

'That's all right, Superintendent Littejohn, but…'

More feet on the stairs. One of the climbers was panting as though overcome by the steps. Mrs. Sandman and Mrs. Hoop entered. It was Bella who was panting; Mrs. Sandman was quite at her ease. Bella put her hand on her copious breast as though ready to have a heart attack.

'When are you going to have a lift put in here, Mr. Ash?'

And then she saw the rest of the visitors. She seemed surprised.

'I thought this was a private meeting?'

'We called to give you all some information. I hope you'll agree to hold the meeting a little later when we've finished.'

Bella put her hand on her chest again.

'Have they got him?'

'Who?'

'The murderer!'

Nobody answered. They had grown used to Bella's outbursts. She was dressed up to the nines, fur coat and all, with all her jewellery scattered about her. Littlejohn couldn't help thinking of her husband, Fred, sitting in his ramshackle office, black rings round his eyes and a suit that looked ready for the ragbag, trying to sort out the bankrupt finances of his firm. He turned to Ash and quietly spoke to him.

'I think you'd perhaps better ring Fred Hoop at the works and remind him that we're waiting for him. That is, if they've not already cut off the telephone.'

Ash went in another room to do it.

Mrs. Sandman, in a less fashionable and expensive fur coat than Bella, looked far better dressed in it.

'What are we all doing here, Superintendent? I thought it was a meeting of the trust directors.'

'I'm sorry to bring you out on a night like this, and I hope you'll not mind putting off the business meeting for a little time. I want to talk to all of you.'

She took it as a matter of course. Very different from Bella, whose scent was fighting a winning battle with the pervading aroma of Mr. Hartley Ash's cigars.

'I can't get any reply from Excelsior. So, Hoop must be on his way.'

Bella's usual husky voice rose sharply. She looked very annoyed.

'Surely Fred isn't coming here. What do you want with him?'

'The same matter we wish to talk over with you, Mrs. Hoop.'

'You're surely not going to arrest anybody *here*?'

More interruptions. First, Fred Hoop, who took an awful time to climb the stairs. He sounded to be carrying a heavy burden on his back, but when he appeared in the doorway, he hadn't even a hat on. The same old clothes, but he'd recently had a shave, which made him look a bit better. When he saw all the crowd of them there, he was acutely distressed. He chose his mother-in-law to address.

'I'm sorry. I didn't know there'd be ladies here. Or I'd have tidied myself up a bit. What's it all about?'

He looked alarmed, as though, somehow, he was going to be accused of villainy, or else the final downfall of Excelsior was about to be sealed and all his work was going down the drain.

'Has something more happened?'

Mrs. Sandman was obviously sorry for him.

'No, Fred. Just sit down and compose yourself. It will be all right. The Superintendent is looking after things and wants to discuss them with us.'

'What things?'

Bella was less merciful. She looked at Fred in disgust.

'Wherever have you been…? And where did you get that suit from? It's a disgrace.'

Poor Fred had no answer and sat down dejectedly. Hartley Ash couldn't make out what was going on. He stood at his desk wondering what to do next.

'Fetch some chairs,' Cromwell said to him. Everyone but Fred was standing around. Ash offered his own armchair to Mrs. Sandman and went off to find the boy, who began to bring in chairs, one at a time, all different, as though he were collecting them from various parts of the building. Finally, they were all seated.

'Are we ready? I wish to know what all this is about and then get away.'

Bella was trying to occupy the centre of the stage, as usual, but her mother, without speaking a word, seemed to dominate it.

'We're waiting for one more visitor, Mrs. Hoop...'

There was no time to say whom. From the noise on the stairs, they all guessed. Someone with a limping gait; a heavy foot on each stair and then a brief pause as the other foot was dragged up. And the thud of a stick punctuating the procession. Alderman Vintner stood in the doorway.

15

ACCOUNT RENDERED

V INTNER WAS PANTING HARD AND LOOKED FURIOUS. HIS LIP
was thrust out and he surveyed the assembled company like
an angry bull wondering which to attack the first.

'What's all this about, Ash? I thought you wanted to see me
privately, not to include me in a public meeting.'

'The police asked me to invite you here, Mr. Alderman.'

Ash licked his lips, like a penitent schoolboy.

'What for? This is a trick.'

He moved across to Tattersall, the man he thought he could
bully, and stood over him.

'Well? You'd better explain before I leave, which I'm going to
do right away.'

Littlejohn intervened.

'I'll take the responsibility, Alderman. It was I who suggested
this meeting. It's to discuss the recent explosion at Excelsior works.
Please sit down. I won't take much of your time.'

'It was you, was it? Somebody's going to pay for this. I don't
propose to waste any of my time here bandying words with you.
I'm going.'

He turned to the door.

'Excuse me, Alderman. Don't go. If you refuse to remain here,
you'll have to accompany us to the police station, which will be
much more embarrassing for you. You have some important

information which the police require. So have the rest of these people. Now, kindly sit down.'

Vintner halted and stood with his back to Littlejohn for a moment. Then he turned, his stick firmly gripped in his fist as though he was ready to rush in to the attack. His neck flushed and the veins on his forehead stood out swollen and livid.

'Right. If you want to make a fool of yourself, now's your chance. Once and for all. Then it will be my turn. I give you five minutes.'

He sat down heavily on the only remaining free chair. Not because he'd been told to do it, but because his leg was obviously paining him through climbing the stairs and then standing about.

'Thank you.'

'Don't thank me. Get on with it.'

Mrs. Sandman was enjoying the little scene. She was smiling faintly as though happy to see Vintner deflated. The alderman caught her eye and glared at her. As for Bella, the presence of so many men affected her considerably. She titivated herself with a small lace handkerchief and Littlejohn felt sure that, if she'd had a chance, she'd have taken out the necessary powder and lipstick and tried to improve her already overdone make-up. She completely ignored Fred Hoop and, having chosen Mr. Hartley Ash as the most likely one to respond, gave him a secret smile.

'Get on with it, then.'

Vintner, torn between keeping his dignity and tearing Littlejohn to pieces, thumped the carpet with his stick. The office boy thought it was a signal that he was needed and rushed in, still holding his comic paper.

'Get out!' shouted Mr. Ash, who was wishing he could follow him.

Littlejohn spoke rapidly and quietly. Vintner watched him with hostile looks.

'Evingden was once a small town of a few thousand people. Then the authorities decided to build a new town and fill it with the overspill of London. The idea was, at first, a dead secret, known only to those negotiating, the London people and the local council. Nevertheless, certain investment trusts suddenly began to buy land in the likely development sites with a view to a very large increase in values when the news became public. Those trusts were the Polydore Trust, the Deliverance Trust and Pook's Retreat Development Company…'

So far, the assembly hadn't taken unusual interest; now they all sat up suddenly, except Fred Hoop, who looked as if he couldn't imagine what Littlejohn was talking about. Vintner was feeling for his stick, ready to rise to his feet.

'I'd advise you to stay, Alderman. This concerns you very much.'

'I've no intention of leaving. It does interest me. I'm wondering what rubbish the police are going to talk about next. I'll have all this aired at the next meeting of the Watch Committee. There'll be a hullabaloo, I can assure you.'

'I can see you're all very interested. Some of you are directors of the various trusts. You, Mrs. Sandman, are perhaps surprised, and your daughter too. You were purely formal directors, receiving good dividends, and probably quite unaware of where they were coming from.'

Mrs. Sandman nodded.

'We were content to leave the finances in the hands of our very competent advisers, Mr. Ash and the late Mr. Roper.'

'Yes, we were. We'd no idea…'

Bella echoed her mother's words and everybody seemed ready to tell her to shut up.

'The improved fortunes of the trusts and the Pook's Retreat Company were due to Alderman Vintner...'

Vintner began to growl.

'Yes, Alderman? I have full proofs of all I'm saying and you had better listen. The mainsprings of the trusts were Alderman Vintner, Roper and the late J. W. Dodd. The alderman obviously couldn't be associated publicly with the trusts. That would have given the game away. So he wasn't a member of the boards, but provided the information and some of the finance...'

Vintner rose and made for the door again, but found Tattersall there with his back to it.

'Move away. I'm going.'

'Not until Superintendent Littlejohn says you may. If you try to leave, I'll arrest you.'

'On what grounds?'

Tattersall didn't quite know, but he took a pot shot.

'Corruption in public office.'

Vintner actually looked relieved. He returned to his seat.

'I'm interested in your charges now. I'll sit this out and then you'll hear from me. Wild horses wouldn't get me away now. Ash... you listening? You're my lawyer, Ash. I shall need you as a witness...'

Littlejohn continued in the same quiet voice.

'It was a precaution, too, against Dodd's and Roper's association with companies buying land in Evingden, to confuse the ownership of such companies. So, the first two companies were owned by the third. A form of remote control which put the inquisitive off the trail. We have then, Dodd spying out and buying available land;

Roper seeking and providing the finance; and, most important of all, Alderman Vintner supplying information acquired in confidence from corporation committees about likely developments of the principal sites.'

Vintner was dead silent. He'd taken out a notebook and was busy writing down points raised by Littlejohn. Now and then, he actually looked pleased and raised his eyes and glanced at Ash as though bidding him to take special note of them. Ash gave him blank looks.

'Mr. Ash, another director, dealt with the legal side of the land purchases.'

Ash looked pleased and relieved, as though he'd done something clever.

'But as the companies' lawyer, he must have been fully conversant with what was going on.'

Ash changed colour and slumped in his chair. He looked almost as ill as Fred Hoop, who was still sitting miserably there as though he were the accused, being tried by the rest.

'And now we come to the Excelsior affair.'

None of the audience, except the police, looked comfortable about it. It was as though they were all well aware of their own parts in the sordid Evingden tragedy and were anxious to hide them.

'A small-town bookie named Scriboma watched the building of a new branch bank from his office windows, and saw the safes arrive as temporary means of holding cash and securities until the strong room could be completed. He knew a man who he thought could easily open those cash safes and he got in touch with him. This friend of Scriboma was suffering from undue interest by the police, but he agreed to try his hand provided Scriboma could obtain the necessary explosive. This didn't deter Scriboma. He knew where and how he could get it. His brother-in-law, Oswald Bugler...'

'Who?'

Fred Hoop suddenly sat up and took notice. The name of Bugler might have been a firework exploding under his seat.

'Bugler. Your cashier at Excelsior.'

'But... Oh, never mind...'

Telephone. That, too, made them all jump again, including Littlejohn. Everyone was on tenterhooks.

'It's for you...'

Ash handed the instrument to Tattersall. There was a brief conversation, mainly at the other end of the line. Tattersall seemed very amused. He scribbled a message on a piece of paper and handed it to Littlejohn.

'Oh dear. We might have avoided this.'

But he didn't tell the rest what it was all about. He handed the note to Cromwell and left the others to wonder.

'To supplement his meagre and uncertain income from Excelsior, Mr. Bugler acted as bookie's runner for Scriboma and almost every week called at Rosealba quarries to collect bets and pay out winnings. Scriboma, who was in a position to blackmail his brother-in-law into doing what he wished, told him to obtain dynamite from the stores there, Bugler managed to steal enough, and more, for the bank job. Scriboma's safe-cracking friend used two sticks of it; Bugler had stolen four. The bank robbery was a miserable flop. Scriboma, left with the remainder of the explosive, held on to it for a while, but a few days ago, hearing that his safe-breaker had been arrested, got cold feet and handed it back to Bugler, telling him to dispose of it.'

Everybody wondered what was coming next, including Vintner who tried to look bored with it all, but didn't succeed.

'Bugler received the dynamite on the morning of the day of the Excelsior explosion.'

'So, it was Bugler who had an accident and blew the place up!'

Vintner looked around for approval at his deduction.

'No. He put the sticks of dynamite in an old box and hid them in the filing cabinet in his office. He intended disposing of them as soon as he could in the safest spot he could think of – the sea. Whilst the explosive was there Bugler had visitors. First, Mr. Tom Hoop arrived. He wanted the time-sheets for checking. They were kept in the drawer of the cabinet in which Bugler had hidden the dynamite, and, as was his custom, Mr. Hoop went straight to the drawer and took out the sheets. He didn't mention the dynamite, and Bugler didn't know whether or not he had noticed it.'

Fred Hoop suddenly awoke again.

'My father was right, then, and all the time I thought he was rambling in his speech because he'd been ill. I hurried him off home. Then…'

'Your father wasn't well when he visited Bugler's office and left with you the enquiry about the dynamite. As he left the works, your father asked you to return the time-sheets to their proper place. You delayed for some time and then you went to Bugler's office. He was out and the cabinet was locked. You held a spare key, opened the drawer, but found no explosive there. This confirmed your view that your father had been talking rather deliriously. Actually, your father did see the dynamite, but between his telling you and your entering Bugler's office, it had been taken by a visitor who arrived between your father's and your own entry.'

Bella sat rigidly in her chair like a pillar of salt. Her mouth was open in stupefaction, too. Vintner had forgotten his notebook. Now he searched frantically for it, found it on the floor and started to hunt for the thread of his narrative again.

'The visitor was Alderman Vintner.'

A great sigh from Bella, as though she'd been principal suspect and was now vindicated. But before anyone else could react, Fred Hoop leapt from his chair, crossed to Vintner and seized him wildly by the throat.

'So, it was you! You swine. I'll…'

The chair on which Vintner was sitting collapsed under the tension of the scuffle, but Fred Hoop still hung on. Finally, Cromwell lifted him out of the wreckage by the seat of his trousers and sat him in a corner on the floor.

'Behave yourself or I'll put the handcuffs on you.'

Vintner sorted himself out of the mess, refusing all help, beside himself with fury. He pointed to Hartley Ash.

'You're my lawyer, Ash. You'll represent me in this affair.'

Ash looked blankly at him, unable to fathom which affair, the assault by Fred or the accusation by Littlejohn.

'I deny that I was in Bugler's office on the day mentioned and your first job, Ash, will be to issue a writ for slander against Littlejohn.'

Littlejohn lit his pipe.

'I have ample proof that you were at Excelsior works and in Bugler's office at the time. I intended Bugler should be here. Unfortunately, he's in hospital. The telephone message was from the police station. Scriboma has beaten up Bugler and is now in gaol himself. But to resume…'

Vintner went to the chair Fred Hoop had vacated and sat on it.

'I'm waiting. You're taking a note of all this, Ash?'

Ash drew a pad and pencil towards him just to show willing.

'You arrived at the main offices at Excelsior to demand from Dodd payment of a large and long overdue account. You were going to threaten him with proceedings which would break the firm. He was your enemy. He was your son-in-law and had treated your daughter very badly. He'd dragged your good name in the mud of Evingden...'

'Never mind my good name. I'm well able to look after that, as you'll soon discover. And keep my daughter out of this.'

'I will. But the domestic quarrel between you and Dodd was very embarrassing to you. He knew all about your premature disclosures of the council's plans for the new town and the development projects which would cause a rise in the land prices which you had bought or caused your friends, including Dodd, to buy. He was in a position to blackmail you. But he didn't choose that way. He decided to make money on his own account.'

Bella was listening with intense concentration to the narrative of Dodd's adventure. She fanned herself with a handkerchief from time to time and smiled now and then, as though Dodd were still alive and she was proud of him.

'It seems to have been the practice for Alderman Vintner to pass on information to Roper, who explored the financial side and then arranged with Dodd to assess the value and attend to the purchase of the properties which would rise in value...'

Vintner remained silent. He wrote something in his notebook and raised his eyes in the direction of Ash to make sure he was noticing what was said.

'One day Roper received information through the usual channels that the corporation of Evingden proposed to acquire the site of Excelsior works for the construction of a bus station. They would pay perhaps £15,000 for it. Roper at once saw salvation in it. The property, including the land, belonged to the Misses Jonas who let it at a nominal rental to Excelsior. There was in the lease, however, an option for the company to buy the property for £5,000. If Excelsior exercised their option and paid £5,000, which Roper would find for them, they'd make a cool profit of £10,000 on the deal. More than enough to repay the company's loan to the Home Counties Bank and relieve Roper of a burden which worried him to death. He told Dodd the news and explained his proposition and together they arranged to by-pass Vintner and put through the deal themselves.'

'All lies! But go on. You're only incriminating yourself more and more in front of witnesses. This will break you, Littlejohn.'

'To return to the day of the explosion. You called to threaten Dodd, Alderman, about an overdue account. When you arrived at the office, he was telephoning. So, you waited outside, unseen and listening to the conversation. It was between Dodd and Mrs. Fred Hoop. I've arranged for Mrs. Hoop and Mrs. Sandman to be present so that there will be no mistake about this. Dodd informed Mrs. Hoop that his wife was going to sue for divorce. Dodd suggested that Fred Hoop might be inclined to do the same, in which case they could...'

Fred Hoop, until then sitting disconsolately in the corner on the carpet, began to struggle to his feet.

'I'll murder Dodd for this,' he shouted; and then he remembered that there was no need to do so. He sank back, put his head between his knees and began to sob. This was a chance for more melodrama from Bella. She rose to minister to him, but her mother seized her by the arm and flung her back in her chair.

'Stay where you are. You've done quite enough to Fred. You ought to be ashamed...'

It was Bella's turn to dissolve into weeping now. Tears ran down her cheeks and made runnels in the deep make-up. Cromwell filled a glass with brackish-looking water from a decanter on Ash's desk and gave it to Fred, who automatically drained it in one. Then he looked surprised at what he'd done.

Littlejohn had to raise his voice above the noise of sobbing.

'As he finished the conversation Dodd told Mrs. Hoop that his fortune looked like being greatly improved through the sale of Excelsior properties. He asked her to meet him at the office at eight o'clock that night as they couldn't discuss the future over the telephone. The alderman had heard enough. He quietly removed himself and went to browbeat Bugler about the account due. In Bugler's office, he saw the drawer of a cabinet open. It contained a box which had once held screws supplied, as the label stated, by a firm of Vintner's trade rivals, Forest and Hedley. Eager to see how Excelsior stock of ironmongery was faring, Vintner opened the box whilst Bugler's back was turned. He found the dynamite. He was in the frame of mind for killing Dodd, but didn't know how. The dynamite gave him an idea. He pocketed it. Then he left.'

'Ha! That's a good one. How did you concoct that bit of cleverness?'

'You told Bugler that you would stop Excelsior credit with Forest and Hedley. How did you know *who* was giving them credit? You'd seen the name when you unearthed the box.'

The sobbing had subsided and Bella was now flashing her tearful eyes in Fred's direction in a manner hinting at reconciliation. Fred's stomach agitated by his too sudden drink of water, revolted... Or it may have been the sight of Bella's approaches... At any rate, he showed urgent signs of being sick, and Ash, anxious about the carpet, rushed him off to an appropriate place and left him there. When Ash returned, he took up his pencil again to reassure Vintner, who, by now seemed to have forgotten all about him. He was inclined to laugh off the situation. He sniggered unpleasantly.

'So you're going to arrest me for stealing dynamite, are you? How are you going to prove it? How are you going to prove anything? I'll deny it. It would be very inconvenient for you if you arrested me just now.'

'No, Alderman Vintner, it will be a more important and serious charge than that. It will be murder. Between Mr. Tom Hoop's arrival in Bugler's office, when he found the dynamite was in the drawer, and Mr. Fred's visit, when he found the dynamite had gone, you had been there. The only other visitor.'

'Very clever and convincing.'

But now Vintner was sweating. He daren't mop his brow and call attention to it and the beads formed a thread which ran off his forehead and down the sides of his fat face.

Littlejohn, too, was perspiring and he daren't show it either. He was luckier than Vintner, however. He could feel the beads running down his back. Much depended on the next few minutes. Tattersall looked bewildered and puzzled and Cromwell knew that the Superintendent was playing a hunch.

'On the night of the crime, you were there, Alderman, at eight o'clock, with the dynamite in your pocket. You thought Dodd and Mrs. Hoop had an assignation in the office. What you didn't know was that Dodd had cancelled it. He'd called, instead, a hasty directors' meeting to arrange for the purchase of their property for £5,000 by the Excelsior company. Or, he might have intended some other slick way of dealing with the transaction to his own advantage. Tom Hoop was too ill to attend; Fred wasn't about, and

Dodd regarded him as a nonentity in any case. He'd called the other two directors, Fallows and Piper, there to form a quorum and start the ball rolling by agreeing to take up the option…'

Bella Hoop started to weep again, this time a loud boohooing, quickly to be silenced by her mother, who pushed her so hard in the back that she almost fell from her chair.

'Be quiet!'

'You determined to dispose of Dodd, and the woman with whom he was betraying your daughter. Also he was planning to double-cross you on one of the biggest of your shady property deals. You had confirmed his betrayal by calling on Roper and bullying out of him what the big deal was that you'd heard about whilst eavesdropping on Dodd's morning telephone call to Mrs. Hoop. I might add, that your treatment of Roper that morning largely contributed to his suicide…'

Vintner seemed unable to control himself further under the weight of evidence and humiliation piling upon him. He rose, his face livid, and pointed his heavy stick viciously at Littlejohn.

'And I suppose now, you're going to say I crept out at night, went in the cellar of Excelsior offices, and blew up the whole place with dynamite. You can't prove a thing. I deny it all. I'm going, and you can't stop me.'

He paused as though waiting for an answer. None came. Dead silence. The outstretched stick slowly performed an arc and trembled to the floor.

It was Tattersall who rose and spoke first.

'Only our forensic experts and the police here know that the dynamite was exploded in the cellar, Alderman. The newspapers and the rest of the public think it was flung in through the window, which sounds a bit more picturesque. How did you know…?'

Another pause. Bella Hoop screamed. Vintner seemed to disintegrate before their eyes. He slowly crumpled from the feet upwards, his eyes staring out of his head, his mouth loose and askew. Then he pitched forward and fell heavily to the floor. At the same time, the door opened and Fred Hoop appeared in the doorway, a sorrier sight than ever.

'Can I go? I'm not feeling so good.'

Alderman Vintner never even faced the charge of murdering three men. He remained in hospital, totally paralysed, for three weeks, and then he died. The police, on examining Vintner's office at the shop, found the remains of the old screw box, torn in many pieces, among the waste paper.

'Why did you have the women at the interview?' Tattersall asked Littlejohn later.

'In the first place, it enabled us to get them all together without much trouble. Vintner thought himself a very clever fellow. In the presence of women, he tried to be more clever than ever. You, yourself, told me he had a reputation for showing off and indiscretion, especially in front of women. He ran true to form and committed his habitual blunder.'

'What would you have done, if he hadn't, but continued to bluff it out?'

'It would have been awkward, but we'd have had to charge and arrest him. There was plenty of circumstantial evidence. We could have made a good case, backed as it was by clear proof of his corrupt practices in municipal affairs.'

'I liked your nerve.'

'Just a hunch he would finally break down... I admired one thing about Vintner. His love for his daughter. He and her brothers insisted on Dodd marrying her after he'd seduced her. Then, Vintner did his best for Dodd. He let him into the secret and partnership of his corrupt practices. And Dodd betrayed him on both counts: his daughter and their shady business association.'

Fred Hoop divorced Bella, who, almost right away became engaged to an Italian count she met on holiday. Fred, with the money from the bus station project, which went through, set up as a local undertaker and married his housekeeper.

Oswald Bugler got away with a fine of £10 for stealing dynamite. Compared with some of the crimes recently current in Evingden, the magistrates regarded Bugler's effort as a minor one. He got himself a job somewhere in Australia, for Mr. Scriboma is in gaol for two years and Bugler doesn't know what mood he will be in when he gets out.

Dear Reader,

We want to tell you about George Bellairs, the forgotten hero of British crime writing.

George Bellairs wrote over fifty novels in his spare time (his day job being a bank manager). They were published by the Thriller Book Club run by Christina Foyle, manager of the world famous Foyle's bookshop, and who became a friend. His books are set at a time when the real-life British Scotland Yard would send their most brilliant of sleuths out to the rest of the country to solve their most insolvable of murders. Bellairs' hero, gruff, pipe-smoking Inspector Littlejohn appears in all of them. Though his world might have moved on, what drove people to murder – jealousies, greed, fear – is what drives them now. George Bellairs' books are timeless.

If you liked this one, why don't you sign up to the George Bellairs mailing list? On signing you will receive exclusive material. From time to time we'll also send you exclusive information and news.

So join us in forming a George Bellairs community. I look forward to hearing from you.

www.georgebellairs.com
George Bellairs Literary Estate

THE BODY IN THE DUMB RIVER

George Bellairs

For the most part, the dead man received public sympathy.
A decent, hardworking chap, with not an enemy anywhere.
People were surprised that anybody should want to kill Jim.

. . .

But Jim has been drowned in the Dumb River, near Ely, miles from his Yorkshire home. His body, clearly dumped in the usually silent ('dumb') waterway, has been discovered before the killer intended – disturbed by a torrential flood.

With critical urgency it's up to Superintendent Littlejohn of Scotland Yard to trace the mystery of the unassuming victim's murder to its source, leaving waves of scandal and sensation in his wake as the hidden, salacious dealings of Jim Teasdale begin to surface.

BRITISH LIBRARY CRIME CLASSICS

The Cornish Coast Murder	JOHN BUDE
The Lake District Murder	JOHN BUDE
Death on the Cherwell	MAVIS DORIEL HAY
Murder Underground	MAVIS DORIEL HAY
The Female Detective	ANDREW FORRESTER
A Scream in Soho	JOHN G. BRANDON
Mystery in White	J. JEFFERSON FARJEON
Murder in Piccadilly	CHARLES KINGSTON
The Sussex Downs Murder	JOHN BUDE
Capital Crimes	ED. MARTIN EDWARDS
Antidote to Venom	FREEMAN WILLS CROFTS
The Hog's Back Mystery	FREEMAN WILLS CROFTS
The Notting Hill Mystery	CHARLES WARREN ADAMS
Resorting to Murder	ED. MARTIN EDWARDS
Death of an Airman	CHRISTOPHER ST JOHN SPRIGG
Quick Curtain	ALAN MELVILLE
Death of Anton	ALAN MELVILLE
Thirteen Guests	J. JEFFERSON FARJEON
The Z Murders	J. JEFFERSON FARJEON
The Santa Klaus Murder	MAVIS DORIEL HAY
Silent Nights	ED. MARTIN EDWARDS
Death on the Riviera	JOHN BUDE
Murder of a Lady	ANTHONY WYNNE
Murder at the Manor	ED. MARTIN EDWARDS
Serpents in Eden	ED. MARTIN EDWARDS
Calamity in Kent	JOHN ROWLAND
Death in the Tunnel	MILES BURTON
The Secret of High Eldersham	MILES BURTON
The 12.30 from Croydon	FREEMAN WILLS CROFTS
Sergeant Cluff Stands Firm	GIL NORTH
The Cheltenham Square Murder	JOHN BUDE
The Methods of Sergeant Cluff	GIL NORTH
Mystery in the Channel	FREEMAN WILLS CROFTS
Death of a Busybody	GEORGE BELLAIRS
The Poisoned Chocolates Case	ANTHONY BERKELEY
Crimson Snow	ED. MARTIN EDWARDS
The Dead Shall be Raised & Murder of a Quack	GEORGE BELLAIRS
Verdict of Twelve	RAYMOND POSTGATE
Scarweather	ANTHONY ROLLS
Family Matters	ANTHONY ROLLS
Miraculous Mysteries	ED. MARTIN EDWARDS
The Incredible Crime	LOIS AUSTEN-LEIGH
Continental Crimes	ED. MARTIN EDWARDS
Death Makes a Prophet	JOHN BUDE
The Long Arm of the Law	ED. MARTIN EDWARDS
Portrait of a Murderer	ANNE MEREDITH
Seven Dead	J. JEFFERSON FARJEON
Foreign Bodies	ED. MARTIN EDWARDS
Somebody at the Door	RAYMOND POSTGATE
Bats in the Belfry	E.C.R. LORAC
Fire in the Thatch	E.C.R. LORAC
Blood on the Tracks	ED. MARTIN EDWARDS
The Murder of My Aunt	RICHARD HULL
Excellent Intentions	RICHARD HULL
Weekend at Thrackley	ALAN MELVILLE
The Arsenal Stadium Mystery	LEONARD GRIBBLE
The Division Bell Mystery	ELLEN WILKINSON
The Belting Inheritance	JULIAN SYMONS
The Colour of Murder	JULIAN SYMONS
The Christmas Card Crime	ED. MARTIN EDWARDS
Murder by Matchlight	E.C.R. LORAC
Smallbone Deceased	MICHAEL GILBERT
Death in Captivity	MICHAEL GILBERT
Death Has Deep Roots	MICHAEL GILBERT
Surfeit of Suspects	GEORGE BELLAIRS
Murder in the Mill-Race	E.C.R. LORAC
Deep Waters	ED. MARTIN EDWARDS
Fell Murder	E.C.R. LORAC
The Body in the Dumb River	GEORGE BELLAIRS
It Walks by Night	JOHN DICKSON CARR
The Measure of Malice	ED. MARTIN EDWARDS
The Christmas Egg	MARY KELLY
Death in Fancy Dress	ANTHONY GILBERT

ALSO AVAILABLE

The Story of Classic Crime in 100 Books	MARTIN EDWARDS
The Pocket Detective: 100+ Puzzles	KATE JACKSON
The Pocket Detective 2: 100+ More Puzzles	KATE JACKSON

Many of our titles are also available in eBook and audio editions